SO
NOT A
POP
STAR

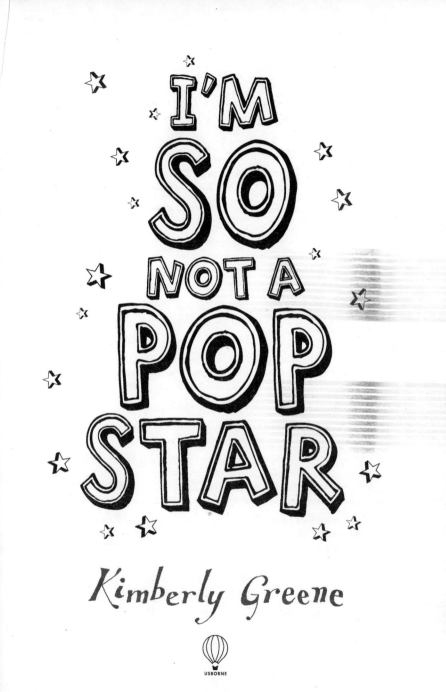

I'M SO NOT A POP STAR

Kimberly Greene

USBORNE

*My thank-yous could fill a hundred pages, but
I'd be remiss if I didn't shout out "Gracias!"
to TG, JG, GW, MRH, RW and AF.*

*With the fullest of hearts, I dedicate this book to Grady
– every day with you is a series of perfect moments
that just keeps getting better and better.
I love you!
I doodle, oodle, oodle, do-oo-oo.*

First published in the UK in 2008 by Usborne Publishing Ltd., Usborne
House, 83-85 Saffron Hill, London EC1N 8RT, England. www.usborne.com

Copyright © Kimberly Greene, 2008.

The right of Kimberly Greene to be identified as the author
of this work has been asserted by her in accordance with the
Copyright, Designs and Patents Act, 1988.

Cover illustration by Stella Baggott.

The name Usborne and the devices ♀⊕are Trade Marks of
Usborne Publishing Ltd.

A CIP catalogue record for this book is available from
the British Library.

JFMAMJJ SOND/08   ISBN 9780746086773
Printed in Great Britain.

CHAPTER 1

Click click click, clack clack click.

Confession Time: I am about to commit a serious blogging blunder. See, *I know* putting too much into a single blog entry makes it tough for the reader to follow. Yet, I trust that MY blog readers are smart enough to handle a big, fat, juicy entry. Of course, I've no idea if anyone is actually out there reading this at the moment, but I know I do have one loyal fan, my BEST friend Olga ("Hellooooo Lady O!").

Sam's *almost*-thirteen-year-old fingers stopped blazing around the keyboard of her beloved, battered laptop. She reached under her desk, around the wastebasket, and into the small nook where she kept a couple of cans of orange cream soda. Her mom's anti-soda rule was majorly non-negotiable, so Sam was careful to keep her stash of treasure carefully hidden. She took one last huge mouthful of fizz, then returned to her typing with such focus, she forgot to swallow.

If your life is as crazy as mine – well, if it is then I feel *really* sorry for you (LOL) – but you'll totally understand why I have so much to discuss today. Here's a quick breakdown of this MAJOR posting:

#1 – I'm *so* wigging out that it's already almost the anniversary of the official start of the *weirdest* year of my life. How often – in a single 365-day period – does a girl have to deal with her big sister becoming a global pop star, her family moving from a tiny apartment to a huge mansion, and her entire life getting put on display in a reality TV show?? (Actually, we've only got the mansion *because* of the TV show.)

#2 – My big sis, Danni, is getting a totally nasty and undeserved public pounding from a new pop singer named Harley. Horrible Harley is dissing Danni in all the magazines, so Danni's upset all the time now, which is seriously uncool.

#3 – Lastly – and SO-NOT-LEASTLY – I'm tickled purple (purple is my fave colour, you know) that FINALLY I've gotten an invite to Olga's family Day of the Dead party!! YES!! I'm off-the-charts excited (even though I don't really know what a Day of the Dead actually is – but I'll find out) because I get to hang with my best friend all day, and the only thing I like better than hanging with Olga is daydreaming about My Perfect Moment. That's this vision I have of me being out in a big field, riding my own horse, at sunset, while eating a waffle cone filled with chocolate-chip-cookie-dough ice cream! Although, now that I'm thinking about it, add in Olga riding next to me on her horse, and there you have it – *total perfection!*

But back to today – you see, the reason it's such a huge deal for me to get invited to Olga's party is because her mom, Giselle Victorio (yes – *the* beautiful, German fashion model) is super-protective and private about her family. Even though I know she likes me, I'm still an "outsider". It's gotten even worse ever since my family got into this wacky reality TV show called *The Devine Life*. Now Mrs. V is always worried whenever Olga and I hang out because of all the video cameras in my house and the camera crew that follows my family 24/7. But even *before* our TV show, Mrs. V wanted to keep her family celebration a relatives-only event; I guess when you have a big family, that makes sense. When it's as small as mine, a "family-only" event means sitting around staring at the same two people you see every breakfast, lunch and dinner.

Sam suddenly remembered that her mouth was full of fizzy orange soda. For a moment, she feared the soda would go up her nose, but she managed to swallow it down. *Man oh man*, she thought, *when I start writing,*

I totally forget about everything else in the world. It's a wonder I don't have to remind myself to keep breathing!

"Calling Samantha. Come in, Little Bit." A piercing voice was zinging out of the intercom. "This is your mother speaking."

Sam rolled her eyes. Duh! *Of course* it was her mom. No one else used the intercom, and even if anyone ever did, no one else on the planet spoke with the same blend of Southern sweetness and *Don't mess with me* steeliness as Rose Devine.

"Sam…?" the voice continued. "You know that your sister and I love you more than anything on this earth, don't you?"

This was odd. Sam crinkled up her nose as she wondered what her mom was going on about.

"Because we are still down here in the dining room, waiting," Rose said gingerly. "No matter how upset you may be, you at least owe us the courtesy of a response."

What? Sam felt as if a heavy brick had just fallen on her head. Her mom was waiting for a response? To what? *Let's see… Today I got up, got dressed, tried to leave for the stables, but Mom ordered me into the dining room for a family meeting – which, of course, was being videoed for our reality show. I went to the dining room: Mom and Danni were there, as was Robert, with his huge, ever-present, icky-white "I'm Danni's super-important music agent" grin. Danni was crying because Harley had said something harsh about her on TV last night. I got the text message from Olga inviting me to her family's party today. I told Mom about the invite, she gave me permission to go, and I raced up here to write in my blog and text Olga. Uh-oh, maybe the meeting wasn't over!*

"Now, Little Bit," Rose continued, "I truly empathize with your disappointment about your sister and I not joining you at the Victorios' today, but still, when I asked if you understood why we couldn't join you, when I explained that the meeting this afternoon was crucial to Danni's career, you could have at least said *something*."

Oh! Sam gritted her teeth. When I asked Mom for permission to go to Olga's *family* party, she thought *our whole family* was invited! She thinks I'm up here because I'm upset that she and Danni won't be at the party with me!

Sam reached up and pressed the "talk" button on the intercom.

"Sorry, Mom!" Sam needed an excuse for running away from the table, but she didn't want to embarrass her mother by explaining that neither she nor Danni were on the guest list. Ah! "I wanted to let Mrs. Victorio know right away how sorry you were not to be able to attend the party today, so I ran up here to send your regrets by e-mail. I *completely* understand that business has to come before playtime, but I knew that you'd want me to let Mrs. V know, because leaving her hanging would be *so uncool*!"

She released the "talk" button and waited for her mother's reply.

"Oh. That's very mature... I'm proud of you for being so responsible, Little Bit." Rose's voice had a tinge of uncertainty in it, as if she wasn't quite sure if her daughter was being genuine or not. "But you know better than to leave the table before being excused; please come back so we can officially finish our family meeting. Mom – out."

Feeling equal parts of relief and guilt, Sam sighed. She wanted to tell her mom that ever since the Devine family had become the subjects of their own reality show, every family meeting had become a painfully

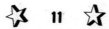

long, ridiculously fancy, mega waste of time. Watching Rose, Danni and Robert pretend to be discussing important stuff, when really they were totally playing to the cameras, was just *icky*.

She sighed and prepared to head downstairs, but then a bell dinged loudly from her computer and pulled Sam's focus back to the screen. It was an e-mail alert from a newstracker that she'd set up to give her a heads-up any time Harley said or did anything newsworthy.

Sam groaned as she read the flashing headline. *Harley Proclaims End of "Puky Princess Pop".*

Sam crossed her fingers in the hope that it wouldn't turn out to be another direct attack on Danni, while reaching for the mouse and clicking on the hyperlink. Immediately, a small video clip appeared. It showed a tough-looking girl with a badly dyed black Mohican and a bunch of nose rings; she was chatting with a handsome young man.

"Hey," Sam cried out at the cute guy, "*Marty Meister!* You always interview Danni! What are you doing with Harley?"

Marty was standing in a studio full of teenagers.

The nasty-faced girl sat on a stool, leaning forward, looking as if she was going to pounce on somebody.

"Ms. Harley Jean Pinkus," Marty spoke directly into the camera, "what was it that motivated you to become a pop singer?"

Harley sneered, "I got sick of all the cheese on the radio. You know, *pointless pop puke* sung by *pretty, pointless, pop princesses* – like Danni Devine! Gag! I turned on my radio and thought that if I heard one more lame song, I'd go mental! So, I wrote a killer song, cut a demo, and now I'm the *real deal*: a pop star who sings from the gut. The day of the *puky pop princess* is over!"

Then the crowd cheered as Harley stormed around the studio singing her hit song, pumping her arms in the air, and giving high fives. The screen faded to black, emphasizing the sound of all those teenagers in the audience chanting, "Harley! Harley! Harley!"

Sam's stomach began to whirl. She hung her head and said a silent prayer that Danni wouldn't hear about this latest attack. Suddenly the bedroom door flew open and Rose Devine scurried in. Wrapping her arms around her daughter, she inadvertently squished

Sam's face against her bosom in one of her super-strong mom hugs.

"Mom!" Sam struggled to get the words out. "Can't…breathe!"

Still hugging, Rose's voice crackled with emotion. "I'm sorry I was so callous, Samantha."

"Mother…" Sam gasped, "…killing me!"

Rose bobbed her head in agreement. "I know, I understand, Little Bit. I do! That's what I wanted to say to you back in the dining room. Lately, the pressure of all this bad publicity and the hurt it's caused Danni has been killing me too."

Sam managed to sputter, "*You're* killing me!"

Rose finally understood. "What? Oh!" She released her daughter. "Sorry! Sorry!" She shook her head. "There's too much going on right now. Your sister is feeling the stress of public embarrassment and it's draining the life right out of me. Please don't be angry with us! I feel awful about not being able to join you at Olga's family thingy today, but we have to do something to rebuild Danni's public image; I'm hoping the meeting today will be a first step in that direction."

Before she could answer, a stupendously loud hunger grumble roared straight out of Sam's belly. It was so noisy that Rose couldn't help but giggle. It snapped her out of her serious mood. She gave Sam an affectionate pat on the head, sighed and stood to leave.

"Little Bit, I want you to go to the party and have a wonderful time. However, you're not allowed outside of this house with a rumbling tummy. Grab a bite before you head off."

Sam nodded. "Will do, Mom, but I don't want to fill up. Olga says there will be tons of food at the party."

Rose strode towards the door. "Well, okay then. Have fun!"

"Thanks, Mom," Sam called out. "Love you."

Turning back, Rose smiled and said, "Love you too, Sam. But if I ever see another can of soda pop in this room, I will put you up for sale on eBay." Then she blew a kiss and left the room.

Sam whipped around and saw the contraband next to her computer.

"*Doh!*"

Gulping the last drop, she tossed the can in the wastebasket and carried on blogging.

My mom ROCKS. As if taking care of Danni and me isn't enough, she also finds the strength to manage Danni's music career – which means she has continual dealings with Super Music Agent Robert Ruebens (blech). Here's a question: why isn't big-shot *Robert* handling this horrible-Harley mess? How can he let somebody like her go on television and say terrible things about Danni? I didn't like it when Danni first got famous and folks on TV said how much they "loved her", but *this*, her being dissed in front of millions of people, this is *sooo* much worse!

Gotta go! I'm off to snag a quick bite to eat and then – Olga's! Can't wait to find out what this "Day of the Dead" thingy is really like. Details soon – PROMISE!

As Sam hit the "post" button to publish her blog on the World Wide Web, she heard a familiar dinging noise. Looking up at the corner of her computer screen, she discovered an instant message from Olga. The tiny text box read:

FROM: LADY O
C U @ my house!!!

Sam typed super-fast. She hit the "send" button and ran downstairs as her reply appeared in the same little text window.

FROM: HORSE GRRL
B there soon!!

CHAPTER 2

Sam manoeuvred her bike around the mess of cars, trucks, people and stuff all over the huge driveway of the Victorio estate.

Olga bounded out of the front door. "Isn't this insane? Not only have *all* my relatives flown in for this party, but I think my mom's got every chef in town cooking in our backyard!"

"You *sure* it's okay for me to be here?" Sam asked in a hushed voice. "I mean, *huge* relief that the camera crew is off following Mom and Danni today, but still, I wouldn't want to do anything to embarrass you in front of all your relatives."

Hooking an arm through one of Sam's, pointed with her free hand. "See that? Over by pool, the person with the insane outfit and the neck wrap of red feathers? Recognize my little sister? Believe me, there's *nothing* you could do that's half as embarrassing as that."

Sam giggled as she watched skinny, gangly ten-year-old Inga Victorio strutting around in a blood-red jumpsuit with a weird scarfy-feathery-thingy floating around her neck.

"What's with the feathers?" she asked.

Olga sighed. "Not sure. Apparently Inga and her little trendoid friends have decided that anything with feathers is *tasty* this season."

"She better be careful of being *too tasty*," Sam giggled mischievously. "From here she looks like a giant red chicken!"

After stashing Sam's bike in the Victorios' garage, the girls race-walked towards the festivities in the backyard and straight over to a long table covered from one end to the other with candy. Sam stared for a moment at all the delicious treats, before realizing that they were all odd shapes – skulls, skeletons, bones, weird stuff. Olga popped a sugar skeleton into her mouth and crunched. Sam reached for one, just as the giant red chicken jumped up in her face.

"Yikes!" Sam exclaimed.

Olga turned to see why Sam yelped. "Inga!" She gestured to the crowd. "You have a hundred aunts, uncles and cousins to pester. Go flap your feathers somewhere else."

Inga ignored her sister; she stuck her nose in the air and waved around the shedding boa. Red feathers flew as she sniffed, "I'm not here to talk to *you*. I'm here to ask Sam if there's any chance *my dearest friend* Danni is going to make an appearance this afternoon." She looked directly at Sam and batted her eyelashes. "Is she? Will she? I so hope so! Danni will totally appreciate my outfit! It's a total pop-star outfit, don't you think?"

Before Sam could answer, Olga pointed across the yard. "Look, Inga! Over by the swimming pool, isn't that Cousin Gabi, wearing the exact same thing?"

"She wouldn't dare!" Inga's face turned as red as her jumpsuit. She stomped off, leaving even more feathers floating around the yard.

Sam whispered to Olga, "How can that girl be so

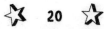

awful to you and in the same breath try to butter me up to get closer to Danni? Does she *really* think I don't see what she's doing?"

"Don't worry. Someday she'll be over Danni and then she'll dismiss you the way she does the rest of the planet," Olga whispered back.

Sam nodded. She forgot about Inga as she turned her attention to the decorations. The Victorios' backyard had been transformed into a party paradise with flowing curtains and flowers. The outdoor fireplace had been converted into a giant altar covered with photos. Everywhere, tables were overflowing with cakes, cookies and other sweets. Coloured flags and streamers had been strung in all the trees. It was a magical scene.

"Here." Olga held out a small bread roll. "You have to try this. It's called *pan de muerto*, the bread of the dead. I wait all year for this stuff!"

The sugary treat melted in Sam's mouth. "Oh!" she exclaimed. "That *is* good!"

Olga reached out and grabbed a mug. "This makes it even better. Try sipping some *chocolate caliente* along with the bread."

The taste of the hot, spicy chocolate drink combined with the buttery, sugary bread immediately became one of Sam's all-time favourites.

"Wickedly yummy!" Sam sputtered. "I can't believe you have this party every year."

Olga nodded as she nibbled on a chocolate lollipop. "Every fall! This and Christmas are my two favourite holidays, but where Christmas is just the one day, we do Day of the Dead for three days. It's about remembering relatives who have died, but I also love how the whole family comes together to remind us to be grateful for every single one of us." She looked across at Inga, who was barking orders at a couple of younger cousins. "Of course, it's easier to be grateful for some relatives than it is for others."

Sam chuckled. "You do have *a lot* of relatives. I can't imagine how it feels to be connected to so many people."

Olga's answer was cut off by her father calling out for everyone's attention.

"Family! *Familia! Damas, caballeros, niños,* please come and join me here at the family altar."

"*¡Hola! Guten Tag!* Hello, everyone." Mrs. V's super-cute accent always tickled Sam's ear. "Thanks to all for being here to celebrate The Day of the Dead or, as my husband says…" She took a deep breath, squeezed her eyes shut, and slowly said, "*El Día de los Muertos!*"

The Spanish-speaking members of the family cheered. Mr. Victorio planted a kiss on his wife's forehead. Sam looked at Olga in confusion.

"Every year my mom practises *for weeks* to give that welcome!" Olga explained. "She's super self-conscious about speaking Spanish in front of my father's family."

Sam nodded. "Oh right. You know, I never really thought about how interesting your family is, with your dad coming from Mexico, your mom from Germany, you being born here in the United States—"

"And, of course, my sister coming from Mars!" Olga said under her breath.

Both Sam and Olga were struggling to keep their giggles under control, as Mr. Victorio continued.

"Today we celebrate *family*. Each of us is special and unique, yet we must never forget that as family, we all share common ancestors—"

Mr. and Mrs. V stepped aside and pointed to the many photos framing the large fireplace. Mrs. Victorio prepared to speak again, but she never got the chance.

The moment was shattered by Cousin Gabi screeching at the top of her lungs. Sam couldn't understand everything she was saying because it was all in Spanish. However, she was pretty sure she heard the words for *music* and *television...* and then *Danni Devine*.

Panic hit like a ton of bricks. *Oh, no! She recognizes me as Danni's little sister! I have to make her hush or Mrs. V is going to mega-blow and then Olga will get totally blamed!*

Sam desperately asked, "Olga, how do you say *shhh* in Spanish?"

With a straight face, Olga replied, "Shhh."

Sam whipped back around. "*Shhh!* Please, Gabi! Yes, I am Danni Devine's sister, but Danni isn't here! Get that? *No Danni!* Please, shhh!"

The commotion got louder. Sam realized it wasn't just Gabi, *all* of Olga's young cousins were jumping, pointing and shouting.

Oh no! Not only were Sam's mom and sister walking across the lawn towards the entire Victorio family, but the camera crew was also with them. Michi, the young videographer, was walking sideways, the camera firmly planted against her eye, somehow managing to look

hip and graceful at the same time. Lou, the sound guy, appeared to be out of breath as he raced alongside and tried to ensure that the microphone he was holding stayed close enough to Rose and Danni so that he could hear whatever they said.

"Sorry, Giselle!" Rose yelled out to Olga's mom. "Sorry! Don't mean to interrupt. Please continue. Everything looks absolutely lovely!"

Inga ran over to Danni. "I'm unbelievably thrilled to see you! You know I'm still your biggest fan!"

Danni enjoyed the attention. "Why, Inga, you always say the sweetest things. That's a lovely scarf."

"It's a boa," Inga gushed breathlessly. "It's *the* accessory of the season!"

"Nice," Danni replied, while smiling and waving to the whole group.

Inga proudly escorted Rose and Danni into the centre of the gathering. She clapped her hands and shouted, "Everyone, I want to introduce our very special guests."

Sam was terrified. *Mrs. Victorio worked so hard to plan this party for* her *family, and now* my *family is stealing the spotlight.*

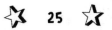 25

"Mom! Danni! Sit over here next to me!" Sam pulled her sister's arm so hard that Danni almost tumbled over. "Mrs. Victorio was just about to say something."

"Oh, I'm sorry, please excuse us, Giselle," Rose exclaimed as she and Danni squeezed in next to Sam. "You go right ahead! We are honoured to be here to celebrate your Deadly Day—"

"*Day of the Dead*," Sam whispered in her mother's ear.

"Day of the Dead." Rose didn't bat an eyelash as she picked up Sam's words and kept on talking. "We are grateful for getting to share this special day with you all."

Mrs. Victorio beamed proudly. She stood tall, took in a breath to say something else in Spanish, but before she could get out a peep...

"Rose! Rose!" A man's voice blared from the front of the house. "Where are you?"

Sam looked at her mother with utter disbelief. *She brought Robert? Robert!? This is the worst day ever. I'll never be invited back here again!*

Rose must have picked up on the fact that Mrs Victorio did not appreciate all the interruptions.

"I am *truly* sorry about this, Giselle," she said earnestly. "Our meeting was cut short, but it had been so dreadful I was too upset to drive, so Robert kindly brought us in his limo."

Mrs. Victorio politely accepted Rose's apology and waited. Once everyone was seated, the ceremony continued, but Sam was only half listening. She couldn't help but look around. It was heart-warming to see old people holding hands with little kids, teenagers leaning against their parents, and babies being handed round for cuddles. At one point, Mr. Victorio called for Olga and Inga to join him and Mrs. V. Sam had never noticed before how much Olga looked like her father. Then, when Mr. Victorio's mother and father walked up and joined hands with their grandchildren, Sam couldn't believe how much Olga looked like her father's father! *Holy guacamole*, she thought, *it's so wild the way three generations of Victorios have matching dimpled chins and the exact same almond eyes.*

Sam glanced over at her mom and sister. It was so obvious that Rose and Danni were mother and daughter. Even though Rose had splendid black hair and Danni's was golden-blonde, the two shared the

same beautiful blue eyes, perfectly shaped noses, and broad, toothy smiles. Sam didn't look a thing like either one of them. Her eyes were green. Her nose looked like a mini baked potato. Her smile was cute, but it didn't seem to bear any resemblance to the rest of her family – that is, the family she *knew*.

Sam remembered all the times her mom had mentioned how much she looked like her father, Daniel Devine. Suddenly, Sam found herself thinking about how much she wished she'd at least gotten to *meet* her father. He had died before she'd been born, so it wasn't as if not having him around was something new.

When it was time to leave, Rose gave Sam a peck on the cheek. "You look exhausted, Sweetie. I want you to ride home with us in the limo. Wait for us in front of the garage."

By the time she reached the garage, Sam only had to wait a moment before the limo backed up next to where she was standing. Rose waved out of the window.

"Come on in, Samantha! Robert will put your bike in the trunk for you."

From inside the limo, a voice whined out, "I'll *what?*"

A loud silence was followed by a scowling Robert stepping out of the back of the limo and holding out his hand for the bicycle. Sam handed him her bike as slowly as she possibly could. She even paused briefly when, out of the corner of her eye, she caught sight of the camera crew filming the moment. Once Robert finally grabbed the bike, Sam climbed into the limo. The trunk slammed shut, Robert got back in, and the engine purred as the driver set off.

Sinking into her seat, Sam began to think back through the afternoon. "Mom?" she asked in a soft voice. "I know that we don't have contact with your side of the family because you all don't get along. I understand that – but what about Dad's family? Are you *sure* there's *no* people on his side?"

Danni stared open-mouthed at her sister. "Wowsa, Little Bit!" she exclaimed. "Where did *that* come from?"

Sam looked out of the window. "I was just wondering…today was so cool, and…it was awesome seeing all the cousins and grandparents and…I…I was just wondering."

"Samantha Sue," Rose said gently, "the past is the past. We have so many blessings in our lives now and even better stuff just around the corner. *You* still haven't told me how you'd like to celebrate your thirteenth birthday! We can do anything you want – throw a party, take a vacation, bake a cake the size of your head!"

Robert looked up for a millisecond before shaking his head and returning his attention to yet another e-mail on his wrist-phone.

Sam's face stayed turned towards the window, but Rose thought she noticed a hint of a smile sneak onto her daughter's lips. She leaned forward and patted Sam's knee.

"If that's not big enough, we can bake a cake the size of *my* head. And if that's still not big enough, we could even bake it the size of *Robert's* head."

Sam swung around and looked into her mother's eyes. "Please, Mom," she begged, "I know this makes you uncomfortable. But if there is *anything* you could tell me about Dad's family that you haven't yet – if there was somebody out there that we could meet – *that* would be the greatest birthday present I could ever hope for. For real!"

Rose looked over at Danni, who looked over at Robert, who looked back at Rose. No one knew what to say.

"Come on, Mom," Sam pleaded. "Isn't there anything you could tell me, any name or place, any picture or old letter, anything that might help us find some relative of Dad's out there in the whole wide world? Please, Mom! Please?"

"*Sam!*" Danni cried out. "Seriously! Get a grip and chill with the whining. You're giving me a headache!"

"Okay, okay." Sam turned to her sister and spoke in a hushed voice. "I'm not *whining*. I'm just *asking*."

Danni flipped a long strand of blonde hair out of her eyes. "Why ask? Mom's told us the story, like, ten billion times. Dad was an orphan who got adopted as a baby. The lady who adopted him died as he was finishing up high school, so he joined the army and then met Mom and they got married and they had me and then Dad died in a car accident just before you were born and that left you and me and Mom." She took a deep breath and gently put a hand on her little sister's shoulder. "Sorry, Little Bit, but it is what it is. There's just us: you, me and Mom. *And that's it.*"

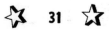

The limo pulled up the long, elegant driveway of the Devine's mansion and stopped in front of the house. The driver got out and walked round to open Rose's door for her. Instead of taking his hand and stepping out, Rose waved him off, reached for the handle, and slammed the door shut.

"Well, that's not *entirely* it," Rose said softly. "There are a couple of details you girls haven't heard."

Sam felt her head begin to spin. *There was more? There really was?*

"Please understand, I haven't shared *absolutely everything* because it was all so long ago and I myself am not clear on how it all fits together, and then time passes and the details get fuzzier and fuzzier. First of all, yes, your father was orphaned as a baby, but Anna Devine, the woman who raised him, didn't *officially* adopt him until she was sick and knew she was close to dying; this would have been when your dad was a teenager in high school."

"Why not, Mom?" Danni asked. "Did it take her that long to decide she wanted to keep him?"

"No, Sweetie," Rose replied gently. "Anna waited because it hadn't been a regular kind of adoption and she was always afraid that someone would come and take him away from her."

Sam piped up. "What do you mean, Mom? I've seen it on TV a million times. A baby is born and at the hospital they hand it over to the adopting parent and it's all good."

Rose exhaled slowly before continuing. "The thing is, Samantha, your father wasn't born in a hospital, he was born on a ship."

"What?" Danni and Sam exclaimed at the same time.

"Yup." Rose nodded. "Dear Anna Devine was on a ship travelling to the United States – she'd gone on a long trip to try and forget how lonely she was after having just lost her husband. When the ship docked in Naples, Italy, a pregnant lady boarded, but just after the ship sailed, the woman died giving birth to the baby – *your father*. It was all very sad. The captain of the ship was going to take the baby back to Italy and give him to an orphanage, but Anna decided fate had brought her and the baby together, so with the captain's permission she scooped him up and brought him home to America with her."

"But…but…but…" Sam had so many questions crashing around in her head, she could barely speak. "Wait! Dad was born outside the country? How could Anna bring home a baby without a passport or birth certificate?"

Rose shrugged. "I guess she just kept making excuses. Remember, back then they didn't have computers or the internet. If a nice, well-dressed woman said the baby was hers and his papers were being mailed, I suppose people believed her."

"But…but…but, Mom," Sam stammered, "what had happened to the baby's real mother? Where was the father? Do you know anything about them?"

"Anna told your father that his birth mother was a pretty lady who spoke German; her name was *Golda*. Someone on the ship spoke enough German to translate what little she shared; apparently Golda was supposed to have been travelling with her husband, but something went wrong. Her husband had gotten lost or hurt. Either way, he was missing, so Golda planned to sail on alone and have the baby in New York, but then the baby, your daddy, decided he wanted to be born early. Golda died in childbirth. Anna was there –

she named the baby Daniel, and brought him to America."

"Golda what, Mom?" Sam was bouncing in her seat with excitement. "What was Golda's last name? How old was she? What was her husband's name?"

"Samantha Sue." Rose placed her hand over her eyes. "Please, I'm begging you, bring down the intensity. This has been quite a day."

Sam bit her lower lip and sat on her hands to control herself. She feared she was going to burst with curiosity.

Rose appreciated Sam's effort to chill. "I'll tell you one last thing, and then let's calm down for now and discuss this later. All right?"

Sam nodded furiously.

"There is a photograph and a ring," Rose said quietly. "Those were the only things of Golda's that Anna ever had – a single snapshot and a simple ring. Those objects were very dear to Daniel."

"Where are they now, Mom?" Sam asked breathlessly.

Rose grimaced. "Well, I'm embarrassed to tell you that I'm not certain: the items are *safe*, I do know that

much. I kept them in a special little blue shoebox. When we moved out of the apartment, Robert hired professional packers and removers to do all the work, remember? Those folks did a wonderful job, but now I honestly don't know *where* that blue shoebox is. I do know it's somewhere inside our house. I've meant to look for the box a million times, but then I'd get busy and something would come up and I'd get distracted, and…" Rose's voice trailed off.

"So…" Sam tried to be sure she understood correctly. "Somewhere inside our giant house is a little shoebox with our only links to our dad's family?"

Rose nodded. Gingerly, she reached out to her younger daughter, but jumped back when Sam practically exploded.

"This is awesome!" Sam shouted. "*I* can find it! I can *totally* find it!"

Before anyone could even try to stop her, Sam was out of the limo, up the stairs, through the front door, and into her bedroom.

CHAPTER 3

Click click click, clack clack click.

It's official: I am RUINED! I'm so sweaty, stinky and gross that even *I'm* disgusted by me! My last three hours have been spent searching the junk-filled attic of this massive mansion for a special shoebox, and I'm sorry to report that things aren't going as I'd expected. You can't believe how big this place is; honestly, it'd take a small army to cover every square centimetre of it! I'm SO not giving up – but for the mo, I am taking a breather.

More when I have something positive to report (hopefully soon!).

As Sam hit the "send" button and waited for her blog to post to the internet, she kicked off her shoes and grabbed a soft, rubbery ball sitting on her desk; she began absent-mindedly tossing it against the far wall of her room. The more she thought about everything – Danni getting grief from Harley, the new info on her father's family, her fast-approaching thirteenth birthday – the harder she threw the ball. This wasn't a problem until, instead of hitting the wall, the ball hit the giant mirror covering a good part of it. The impact made a terrible sound.

Instinctively, Sam's hands flew up to cover her eyes, but instead of the sound of shattering glass, there was a creaky, clanky noise as the whole wall started sliding up and in, like a garage door. She peeked through her fingers in time to see first the feet, then the legs, next the arms crossed over the chest, and finally the irritated glare of a large, dreadlocked TV director.

Sam tried to ignore the displeasure on the face staring down at her. "Good evening, Blu," she chirped.

"How's things in your world?"

"Oh, no, Miss Thing," came the reply. "You do not almost shatter my very expensive, super-secret, mirrored-control-room door and then try to make it good by acting all cute."

Sam saw enough of a glint in Blu's eye to know that he wasn't *really* mad.

She bowed her head. "Then Mr. Malcolm Bluford, king of all directors in reality television land, please accept the apology of the unworthy little Devine standing before you."

Blu regally raised his left eyebrow. "That's better." He tossed his dreadlocks over his shoulder before breaking out into his usual huge, warm grin. That smile, however, vanished as he got a whiff of a very sweaty, stinky Sam. "Whoo, girl, you *seriously* need to be thinking about getting yourself into a shower!"

Any other time, Sam would have laughed at Blu's comment, but she was so shattered and mega frustrated about her lack of progress in the search for the box, that she grimaced and looked down at the ground.

"Hey, girl." Blu was so surprised by Sam's reaction

that he forgot himself and began to walk towards his young friend. "I was just—"

"Stop!" Sam called out as his foot stepped onto the ledge between her room and his office.

"Whoops." Blu caught himself and hopped back. "That was almost bad."

Blu's mellow response annoyed Sam. She knew his TV director contract made it clear that he was not to have contact with any of the Devines; this was to make sure the family's reality show stayed *real*. Sam thought it was plain silly. Over the past year, no matter how unreal life had become – with sudden fame and fortune – Blu had been the most real person in her world. He'd consistently remained her friend, practically her big brother. "You getting fired would not be *almost bad*," she said with an edge in her voice, "it would be *disaster-movie bad*."

Blu pulled over his chair and sat down. "What's up with you?" he asked. "Why the drama? You aren't this upset by what I said about you being smelly."

"No," she said shaking her head, "I'm all frustrated trying to figure out how…" Sam paused, realizing she'd have to explain *everything* about this crazy day to Blu,

otherwise he'd never understand the unimaginable importance of the shoebox. Unless…

"You haven't been watching the live video today have you," she asked hopefully.

Blu pretended not to understand. "What live video?"

Sam pursed her lips and gave him her best *Give me a break* stare.

Smiling, Blu continued. "Oh, you mean the live video feeds of your life playing out that I *have* to watch each day as part of my job?"

Sam playfully stuck her tongue out at him.

Blu turned his head away. "Excuse you, Miss Thing. Not only is that unattractive, but keep it up and I won't tell you how you've already solved your own problem."

"Huh?"

Standing tall and saluting, Blu barked, "General Devine, you've done a masterful job of assessing the situation."

Sam's blank face matched the blankness in her brain. "Huh?"

Blu pointed to one of the many video monitors filling his control room. This particular screen showed a close-up of Sam's blog. Holding out his hands to

frame the screen, he read loudly and slowly, "It'll take a small army to cover every square centimetre of this place." He waited for her to catch on; when she didn't, he spoke slowly: "'A small army'! You need 'a small army'!"

Sam sighed. "And…?"

Blu slapped his head. "And *think*! Where could you find a small army, or better yet, a *small* army of *small* people. Where were you this afternoon?" He waved his hands in the air, trying to get Sam to pick up on his idea.

"OH!" She got it. She ran out of her room, but then ran back in and gave Blu the biggest smile he'd seen in a very long time.

"You rock!" And then she ran back out of the room.

Exhausted, Blu fanned himself with his hand as he slowly lowered the giant mirror. "…Getting too old for this!" he said, to no one in particular.

Sam leaned over the edge of the banister and yelled down, "Mom! Mom!"

She bolted down the grand staircase and around the ground floor of the mansion, calling for her mother. Finally Sam looked outside, where she saw her mom and Robert sitting at a table, looking over a pile of papers, while Danni floated on a raft in the pool nearby.

Sam ran over and plopped down in a chair. She gave her mom her sweetest grin before asking, "Mom, would it be okay if I invited a friend, or two… uh, a few friends over for dinner tonight? Please?"

Rose tried to smooth Sam's hair. "If your friends wouldn't mind salad and frozen pizza, then that's no problem at all."

Sam gave Rose a quick peck on the cheek. "Thanks!" She turned to face her sister. "Um, Danni? You're going to be home for dinner tonight, aren't you?"

Raising her arms to stretch and yawn, Danni nodded. "Yeah, I guess. We had such a crazy day, a quiet night sounds heavenly."

Sam raced back to her room. She plopped back down into her desk chair and opened an instant message window on her computer desktop.

FROM: HORSE GRRL
TO: LADY O

Your cousins want more time with a pop star?
Call me!!

It was only a few seconds before the phone rang.

Sam told Olga her plan and Olga agreed it was brilliant.

One hour later, Sam heard the doorbell.

Robert opened the door and found himself staring down at twelve almost-teenagers. He tipped his head back and yelled, "Rose!"

Sam came flying down the stairs.

"No prob, Robert. I've got this."

She led the group up to her bedroom. Once there, Sam explained everything in English and Olga translated into Spanish so that all her cousins could understand.

"First, thank you all oh-so-much for coming tonight," Sam began.

One of the cousins spoke up. "Danni *will* be here for the dinner, yes?"

Sam nodded. She felt kind of guilty, but if she had to trade a little time with her sister to get the assistance she needed, it was worth it. She secretly prayed that

Danni would feel the same way and not get too mad at her for this.

The group split into teams; each team had at least one person with a cellphone and a specific part of the house to explore. Olga and Sam stayed in "command central" (Sam's bedroom) to coordinate. Every couple of minutes or so, Olga would text each team to get a status report. The first hour went by painfully slowly, but then loud, squeally noises blasted out of Olga's cellphone. The Green Team had found the box! Olga ordered everyone to meet in the living room.

As all the girls gathered downstairs, Rose and Robert were entering the living room as well; they were in the middle of yet another discussion about the best way to deal with the latest public insults coming from Harley. Rose was rather surprised by the number of young girls filing into her living room, but when she saw one girl set a small blue shoebox on her coffee table, she understood immediately what Sam had done. While she was a tad uncomfortable with the thought of strangers going through her belongings, she couldn't help being impressed with her daughter's ingenuity.

Sam caught Rose eyeballing the shoebox and held her breath as she waited for her mom's reaction.

Rose hushed Robert and invited all the girls to sit. Robert had no idea what was going on and made no attempt to hide his annoyance at being ignored. He tapped his fingernails loudly on a side table at the back of the room, but nobody took any notice of him.

"Ladies, it was very sweet of you all to come over and help Sam," Rose said, looking round at everyone. "This is a very exciting moment for her, for our little family. So Danni should be in here before we open the box. Samantha, would you please get your sister?"

Sam nodded. She raised her head and yelled at the top of her lungs, "DANNI! Mom wants you in the living room, NOW!"

Rose closed her eyes and shook her head, but she didn't say a word.

Danni scurried in. "I'm here, I'm here." Seeing all the Victorio cousins, she guessed that they'd come to be near her. "Oh. Nice to see you all again. Listen, I thank you all for being such awesome fans, but I'm super tired and..." Noticing the box in the middle of the table, Danni's mood immediately warmed up. "You brought me a present?"

Before anyone could correct her, Danni reached over and opened the box. Sam, Olga and every one of the Victorio cousins gasped.

Danni stared into the box. "Wow. Okay, I really appreciate this…" She offered a sweet, yet befuddled smile to the girls. "…this awesome picture of…" Danni was clueless. "I'm sorry, you all, I don't get it."

Sam leaped over and stared down at the contents of the box: a tattered photograph and a simple silver ring. She lifted both items and carefully laid them on the coffee table. Everyone crowded round to get a look, as Sam turned to Danni and exclaimed, "These aren't gifts for *you*! They're for *us*! This is *the* shoebox, the one Mom told us about in the limo today! This picture is of our dad's *real* parents! This is our grandma and grandpa!"

That got Robert's full attention. He snapped up the photo.

"Let me see that!" He studied it intently. "Hmm… You know, Rose, these are good-looking people. Tabloid magazines *love* this long-lost-family-revelations

stuff. This could be exactly what we need to get Danni some positive press coverage."

"I don't think so," Sam snapped, as she reached to take the photo from Robert. Danni, however, snagged it first.

She stared at Robert. "I'd like to see it for myself before we show it to the whole wide world." She held it in front of her. "It is interesting, and Sam, the woman looks a *tiny* bit like you, but honestly, I don't really see what it's got to do with *us*. We won't ever know anything about these people. They're from a whole other time and place. It's not like we can call them and go over for Sunday lunch. We don't even know their full names."

Olga's cousin Gabi had been quietly sitting against the wall, watching Danni, but as Danni held up the photo, her focus switched to the picture. Something obviously caught her attention as, shuffling over, she ended up nose-to-picture-to-nose with Danni. Suddenly, she let out a piercing shriek that caused everyone, even Mr. Cool-as-a-Cucumber Ruebens, to practically jump out of their skin. Then she babbled something in Spanish and all the Victorio cousins began murmuring with excitement.

Sam watched and waited until she couldn't stand another second. "What?" she begged Olga. "What's going on?"

"Sam…" Olga shook her head in amazement. "You are *never* going to believe this!"

CHAPTER 4

Click click click, clack clack click.

I have news to tell you that is more exciting than anything – EVER!

NOTE: If you are drinking something, put it down so my super-exciting news doesn't make you squirt it through your nose.

I'm almost certain (like 99.999%) that I now have a photo of my dad's mother and father AND I think I know their names! Whoa, I'm so excited

I'm getting all dizzy; time to slow my roll. (*Big deep breath.*)

Okay, I'm better. Now, here's what just happened:

Olga's cousins helped me find THE shoebox. Inside there was a really old photo. Olga's cousin Gabi saw something on the back of the picture and realized there were names written on it. Not just random names, but typical names of people from Poland (Abraham + Golda Zabinski). From *Poland*! You might wonder how a girl from Mexico would know about Polish stuff (I did). Turns out Gabi's grandma comes from Poland. I admit that I expected the names to be German, because Mom told me that my dad's birth mother spoke German, so I'm more than a little confused… But whatever, a clue is a clue and I'm following it!

It took for ever for Olga's cousins to eat their pizza and get their picture taken with Danni, but,

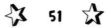

finally, everyone has gone. I'm in my room searching the web for more pieces to this puzzle of my dad's family history. I think I've found something; here are the *exact* words written on the back of the old photo:

Abraham + Golda Zabinski – 4 Lutego 1954, Föhrenwald

Wikipedia shows that *Lutego* is the Polish word for February. So *4 Lutego 1954* is Polish for February 4th 1954. THAT must be the date that this picture was taken! Maybe it was someone's birthday, or even their wedding day! Wouldn't *that* be the wildest thing ever – if I were holding my grandparents' wedding picture?!? I might be stretching on this – it's not like the man and woman appear to be wearing anything fancy – but still, way back in 1954, pictures were super-expensive (that's what my mom said). Plus, the man and woman both have a total gleam in their eyes; put it all together and I'm pretty sure I'm right: this photo WAS taken on a very special day!

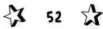

Here's something that has me way confused. My search of the word *Föhrenwald* keeps giving me websites about "displaced persons camps" in Germany. It seems that at the end of World War II (I know it's a majorly long time ago but we're talking about grandparents, so it makes sense that we'd have to deal with history, right?) many people had lost their homes and had nowhere to go, so they ended up living in these mini-towns made up of tents. It doesn't sound like any of the camps I've heard of; there was no canoeing or horse riding. There was a lot of waiting to see if any family, who'd gotten lost in the war, would come and find you. Even though the war ended in 1945, there were still people living in these camps all the way up to 1957!

I wonder if Golda and Abraham were in this camp and got married there? Oh! Almost forgot! In the box, along with the photo, was a tiny ring. It's not fancy, but it looks like the ring Golda's wearing in the picture, so I'm thinking that this might be my grandma's wedding ring! I begged to put it on a chain and wear it round my neck, but Mom said no; she didn't want to chance it getting lost. (sigh)

Sam hit "send" and reread her blog as it posted. There was a part of this story that wasn't making sense. Needing someone to bounce her thoughts off, she scooted her chair over to the giant mirror, smiled her cutest smile, and tapped gently.

"Oh, Mr. Bluford," she cooed.

"I'm eating."

"Aw, come on, Blu," Sam whined. "I really need to talk. Please?"

There was a long pause that Sam filled by tapping, waving and grinning into the mirror. Eventually, Blu caved; the mirror slowly rose out and up.

He struggled to twirl a big mouthful of spaghetti onto his fork. "Talk fast; I have to go to a meeting." He saw the disbelief on Sam's face. "The production team meets every night to plan how best to cover you crazy Devines the next day."

Sam hopped up from her chair. "You remember World War II, right?"

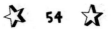

Blu choked mid-swallow. "Either you need a history lesson or an eye test! How old do you think I am?"

"No!" Sam laughed. "I didn't mean *do you remember* as if you were there! I know you're way too young. I meant do you remember as in from history class, do—"

"Chill, my little friend." He cut her off. "Yes, I've heard of the Second World War."

Sam got down to business. "Did you read tonight's blog? While I was typing it, I mean?"

Blu gave a quick thumbs up as he chowed on another mouthful of pasta.

"So you know about me guessing that the picture might be a wedding photo and that Golda and Abraham may have been in that weird camp place?"

Again, Blu signalled *yes* as he chewed.

"I don't know enough about that time in history to answer all the questions in my head, so I thought that by asking someone older…" Sam was very careful with her words. "…someone *more educated* than myself, I might be able to figure out some holes in my guesswork."

"Go for it." Blu nodded as he glanced at his watch. "I'll answer as many questions as I can in the next four minutes. Then I'm outta here."

"Cool beans." Sam clapped her hands together. "Okay, if my dad's mom and dad had Polish names, why was Golda speaking German? This isn't making sense to me. I mean, if you have a Polish name and you write in Polish, wouldn't you *speak* Polish?"

"Uh…right." Blu looked away.

Sam could see that he obviously knew something that he wasn't sharing with her.

"What?" she pressed. "What don't you want to tell me?"

Blu shook his head. "Look, Sam, I'm not a teacher. I don't want to say something that's going to be too much for you to deal with."

Sam rolled her eyes. "Please! Over the past year, you have never had a problem telling me anything. You're the best grown-up I know for explaining stuff everyone else thinks I'm too young to understand."

Blu wished there was more time, but he only had two minutes before he *had* to leave for his meeting. "Remember, I could be wrong about this. I'm giving you my best guess based upon all the information we have – get me?"

"I get you, already! Talk!" Sam cried out as she sat in her chair, ready to listen.

Putting down the spaghetti, Blu wiped his mouth and swallowed hard. "Okay. It sounds like maybe your grandparents *had* to leave Poland and ended up in a camp in Germany – where they learned to speak the language – because *maybe* they *might* have been Jewish."

Blu waited for Sam's reaction.

She looked down at the ground and then back up at him. "I don't get it."

"What don't you get?"

"The Jewish thing," she replied. "Where'd *that* come from?"

Blu snapped his fingers as he remembered something. "You wrote in your blog a while back that one of your favourite books is *The Diary of Anne Frank*, yes?"

Sam nodded.

"Why were Anne and her family hiding?" Blu asked gently.

Sam answered matter-of-factly. "They were hiding because they were Jewish, and the Nazis were trying to round up all the Jews and send them to *work camps*, not to *displaced person camps*."

"Yeah, *during* the war," Blu explained. "But where would she have gone after the war? What if she'd survived? Would she have had a home to go back to?"

Sam began making connections. "Oh, so this could mean that my grandpa and grandma might have been in hiding like Anne Frank?" Sam began to pace the room. "So this could mean that I might be a little Jewish. I could have a real connection to one of my favourite authors. I could have more in common with Anne Frank than just being a girl who likes to write!"

"Sam," Blu called out as he began to lower the giant mirror, "I really have to run now. I've got *just* enough time to climb down the back stairs and get to my meeting. I promise we'll talk more later."

"But I have so many more questions!" she called out, trying to keep eye contact with Blu by lowering herself to the ground with the mirror. "I have no idea what it means to be Jewish, even just a little!"

"No one on the production team will be much help – Michi is a Buddhist, Lou is Catholic, and I'm a Baptist," Blu explained just before the mirror touched the ground. He grabbed the microphone as he was running out of the back door of his control room and managed to get out one parting thought: "Try Robert."

Sam's heart dropped. *Robert?* she thought. *Try Robert? Robert?* A horrifying idea hit her. *Is Robert Jewish? Does that mean I could have something in common with him? Oh no! This doesn't mean I could possibly be related to him, does it?*

Determined not to think about any connection between her and her arch-enemy for the moment, Sam threw herself into her chair, scooted over to her desk, and started doing some more research. She checked website after website for information on displaced persons camps. Even though it was now way past her bedtime, Sam was so pumped with the idea of learning more about her family that she had both the energy and the focus to work all night.

Suddenly, that focus was broken by Rose knocking at her door.

"Little Bit?"

The interruption startled Sam so much that she jumped and banged her knee against the bottom of her desk.

Rose peeked her head in. "It's awfully quiet up here. Everything all right?"

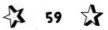

Wincing in pain, Sam turned in her chair and nodded. "It's all good, Mom, all good."

The relief in Rose's voice was *way* obvious. "Happy to hear that. I was worried that the drama – the story, the photo, today's party – that it would be too much for you. Family history stuff can be very emotional. Your dad rarely discussed any of it because it always made him choke up, and for someone as smart and sensitive as you...well, I'm proud of how you are handling everything. Now, Honey, it's time for you to hit the hay."

"You got it, Mom. I'll be in bed in ten minutes."

"Sounds like a plan, Sweetie." Rose walked over and kissed her daughter on the forehead. "Goodnight. Sleep tight. Don't let the bed bugs bite."

Sam nodded, swivelled back to the screen and typed away, as Rose shut the door behind her.

I love the internet! Already, I've found over a hundred websites and groups that might give me more info on Abraham or Golda. I'm hoping to learn something specific (ANYTHING – where they were born, if they had brothers or sisters...)

so badly that I'm crossing all my fingers and toes (I'd cross my eyes too but I'm afraid that Mom's threat about them sticking that way will come true).

Goodnight, my friends! Hey – if you want to cross your fingers and toes for me too, I'd really appreciate it!

TTFN!
Sam

CHAPTER 5

After the craziness of the previous day, and dry eyeballs from five more hours of internet searching before she'd gone to bed – despite her promise to her mom – Sam needed to get to the stables and spend some quality time riding her favourite horse, Thunder Bay. Once she'd had a bit of a lie-in to recover from her late night, she got herself up and dressed. Bounding down the grand staircase and into the kitchen, she practically ploughed right into her mom.

"Whoa, cowgirl!" Rose exclaimed as she jumped aside. "Nice to see you in such fine fashion." She leaned against the kitchen counter and smiled.

"Samantha, having all those girls help you find that old shoebox was genius. I want you to know how impressed I am with how you set a goal and then found a way to achieve it."

Sam, busy wolfing down her cereal, didn't hear a word. She held the bowl up to her mouth to slurp down the last bit of milk, but because she was rushing so much, ended up spilling most of it down the front of her shirt. She looked down at the mess and paused for the briefest moment before simply rubbing it in with her hand.

Rose was horrified. "*Excuse me?*"

Sam giggled. She knew that, even though it drove her completely nuts to watch Sam leave the house in a less-than-perfect state, Rose wouldn't make her change into clean clothes just to go riding. She leaned over and gave her mom a quick peck on the cheek before racing to the door.

"Oh sure," Rose teased, "disgust me and then leave me with that pathetic excuse for a goodbye kiss."

When Sam turned back and saw the glint in her mom's eye, she couldn't help but giggle. Playfully, she shuffled over and was about to plant a huge kiss on her

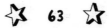

mom's cheek, when she heard Robert entering the mansion, bellowing out that he and Rose had to leave for a big meeting in thirty minutes. Sam froze. She remembered what Blu had said to her last night when she wanted info. *Try Robert.* And then she thought, *I have no idea how to even talk to that guy.*

Robert strolled into the kitchen, poured himself a cup of coffee, sat at the table, opened up the newspaper he'd carried in, and proceeded to immerse himself in his reading. Sam studied him before plopping herself down in the chair directly opposite him.

"Um, Robert?" she asked.

The newspaper remained up as he responded with a disinterested, "What?"

Sam made a superhuman effort to be sure her voice was kind and positive. "I was just wondering…" She had to think up a clever way to find out if Robert really was Jewish and could be a source of information for her, without him *knowing* that that was what she was doing. If he had any clue, he'd be sure to make her pay dearly for bothering him. "I was wondering when was the last time you went to church?"

Sam sat back in her chair, feeling rather proud of

herself. She'd come up with a question that would get her the info she needed without being too obvious.

The newspaper lowered slowly onto the table, revealing a bewildered Robert Ruebens. He looked over at Rose for some understanding.

Equally surprised by the question, Rose shrugged her shoulders and waited to see where Sam's bizarre conversation was heading.

"See, I was just wondering…" Sam tried to act as if the whole topic was no big deal. "We haven't been in a while so I thought maybe we could go with you one Sunday."

The newspaper went back up as Robert replied, "I don't go to church."

"Why not?"

"Because I don't."

"But why don't you?" she pushed.

"Because I'm Jewish." Robert dropped the paper onto the table. "And as a Jewish guy, I go to temple on Saturdays, not church on Sundays. *Okay?*"

Sam was so excited to have found a Jewish person to address all her questions to that she leaned back in her chair. Unfortunately, she leaned a bit too far and

the chair tipped over. Sam landed flat on her back on the kitchen floor. Rose raced over.

"Samantha Sue!" Rose sputtered as she helped her daughter up off the kitchen floor. "What in the world is with you this morning? First you pepper Robert with odd questions and—"

The house phone started ringing. Sighing, Rose waved her hands in the air. "I'll get it, I'll get it. I can't remember what I was saying anyway." Shaking her head in exasperation, Rose glanced about and realized there were no handsets in the kitchen. She growled in annoyance and stomped into the living room to find one.

Sam turned her full attention back to Robert. Grabbing the fallen chair and setting it upright, she threw herself into it, leaned forward with her elbows on the table, and let her eyes bore into Robert.

"So, being Jewish means you don't do church on Sundays, huh? What else don't you do?"

Dropping his paper onto the table, Robert gave up any hope of reading. He paused before answering her flatly. "Christmas."

"What?"

"I don't *do* Christmas."

Sam didn't understand. "But you came to our Christmas party last year."

Standing to escape the barrage of questions, Robert glared at Sam. "Here's a newsflash for you, kid. One need not celebrate the religious part of Christmas to go to Christmas parties and eat Christmas cookies. I do not have time to be your Sunday-school teacher. You want a crash course in being Jewish? Go to Marshal's."

Sam hopped up to stop him. "Where? Who's Marshal?"

"Marshal's Deli." Robert sighed in exasperation. "It's the best delicatessen in town. Don't kids today know anything besides pizza?"

There was an uncomfortable silence, as if Robert was expecting Sam to say something. She had no idea how to respond and simply stared back at him.

"A deli," he eventually growled, "is a cross between a fast-food joint, a grocery store and a restaurant. People go there for big sandwiches and matzo-ball soup. Now, go away; I've wasted enough time on you for one morning."

Sam wanted to ask Robert more. However, the disturbed expression on her mom's face as she returned to the kitchen made Sam freeze. *Uh-oh*, she thought, *there's no way this is good.*

Rose's eyes were freakishly wide open, as if she'd just seen a ghost, but her jaw was clenched, like she was mad at that ghost. She walked over, sat at the table, and spoke without making eye contact with either Sam or Robert. "Please," she said in an eerily calm voice, "please, join me here at the kitchen table. Get Danni here, too."

Sam bolted out of the kitchen and raced up to her sister's room. Once there, she struggled to both breathe and convey the urgency. "Hurry!" (Puff puff.) "Need you in the kitchen." (Pant pant.) "*Now!*"

Danni was sure Sam was being melodramatic, but she followed her little sister downstairs.

"Okay, Rose," Robert said as the girls entered the kitchen, "everyone is here."

With an odd expression on her face, Rose cleared her throat and spoke. "I just had a *very* interesting conversation. The International Red Cross called to double check some of the information *I* submitted

 68

online with *my* official inquiry about my husband's birth parents."

Danni and Robert both appeared completely puzzled. Sam, on the other hand, began chewing her lower lip; she put her head down and kept her eyes glued to the floor.

"Samantha Sue Devine," Rose said in a soft but stern voice, "I need to know *exactly* what you did."

Without looking up, Sam began confessing at light speed how, the previous night, she'd stayed up and surfed the web and found out about Föhrenwald being a displaced persons camp and that Zabinski was both a common Polish name and also a Jewish name and how that had led her to a website about places that helped people find missing relatives who got separated in wars and ended up in those displaced persons camps and how as she was filling out the e-mails to look for information on missing relatives she knew better than to give out her name or number, but since she was *so* hoping someone would get back to her, she gave Rose's name and phone number, and she knew it was wrong and she promised *never ever* to do it again!

Before another word could be spoken, Robert's fancy wrist-phone began buzzing.

"Rose," he said, "our meeting with the T2CT live concert promoter is across town. We need to leave immediately."

Watching her mom nod at Robert before looking at Sam with those *I'm disappointed in you* eyes, Sam's heart felt like it broke into a million pieces. There were few things in life that hurt Sam as much as knowing she'd truly let her Mom down.

Rose, in turn, noticed the pained expression on her younger daughter's face. She put her hand on Danni's shoulder and whispered, "I need you to spend some time with your little sis today."

Danni whispered back, "Sure, Mom. I got ya."

Rose silently mouthed, "Thank you." She turned to leave, but stopped before stepping out of the kitchen. "Samantha Sue," she said gently, "we'll discuss everything when I get home. Don't worry, I'm not *that* mad at you."

The two sisters remained motionless until the sound of Rose's heels clicking on the floor became so faint, it was clear that she and Robert had left the mansion.

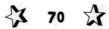

Then Danni threw her hands in the air and gave an order.

"Samantha Sue, go get changed! The Devine sisters are going out for brunch!"

"No thanks," came the soft, sad response, "I'm meeting Olga at the stables soon."

Danni grabbed Sam's cellphone. After a couple of quick taps on the tiny keyboard, Danni put the phone back into her sister's pocket.

"I've sent a text informing Olga that you've been detained and will join her at the stables after brunch."

Sam protested, but Danni pushed her out of the kitchen and up the stairs.

"No whining," she commanded. "You will go to your room, put on a fabulous outfit, and meet your even-more fabulous sister at the front door in ten minutes!"

Still smarting from the scene with her mom, Sam slunk off to her room. As she dressed, the same three thoughts kept spinning round her brain: *I can't believe Mom didn't kill me, I wonder if Mom is going to kill me later,* and *did the Red Cross call back so fast because they thought they might have some info for us?*

As always, Sam was dressed before Danni. She knocked on her sister's door.

"Almost there," Danni hollered. "Meet me at the front door in a minute."

Sam turned and hopped down the stairs. She plopped onto the bottom step to wait.

"Ta-da!"

Danni stood at the top landing in a fancy pose. Sam wanted to burst out laughing at her sister's crazy outfit. Danni's red dress had yellow fringing all over it. She was carrying a sort of brown, wrinkly, shapeless clutch bag, and the whole ensemble was topped off with one of those funny, feathery boa things that Inga had been wearing at the party.

Danni carefully descended the staircase. When she reached the front door, she spun around slowly to give Sam a 360-degree view of her wonderfulness.

"What's with the fringe?" Sam asked. "And is that thing under your arm a handbag or are you bringing a packed lunch to brunch?"

"This –" Danni held out the bag – "is *the* clutch bag of the year." She sighed dramatically. "It's sad how little you know about fashion."

"Oh, I know fashion," retorted Sam, puckering her lips and strutting out of the front door like a crazed supermodel.

"Yikes!" Danni laughed. "I won't say another word about you dressing like a slob if you *never* make that face again. Deal?"

Sam held out her hand. "Deal – *if* you let me pick where we go for brunch."

"Sure." Danni shook Sam's hand before walking over to her car. She slipped behind the wheel of the pink convertible and backed it up until it was directly in front of Sam. "I was going to let you decide anyway," she said with a twinkle in her eye. "So, here we are; the only thing standing between me and some food is your decision."

Sam threw herself into the car. Pointing forward, she exclaimed, "Marshal's Deli!"

Danni stared at her little sister in disbelief. "You can't be serious!"

"What's wrong with Marshal's?"

"Only old people go to delis!" Danni moaned.

"Please take me to the deli, Danni!" Sam begged. "I'll totally make it up to you. Besides, if only old

people go, no one will recognize you there! We could have an entire meal without fans bugging you for your autograph. Wouldn't that rock?"

"Oh, all right." Danni caved. "But sometimes, Little Bit, you really are a weird kid."

Sam giggled. "That's a weird *almost-teenager*, thank you!" She buckled her seat belt and leaned back. It was a beautiful day. She was riding around in a convertible, going out for brunch with her sister, at a place where she hoped to learn some cultural stuff about her newly discovered family. *This is one of those practically perfect moments you only read about in books*, she thought, as the car zoomed out of the driveway.

Sam was too busy enjoying herself to notice Michi and Lou running around from the back of the house with all their video and sound equipment, and jumping into a Jeep.

CHAPTER 6

The Devine girls entered the deli, and as Sam had predicted, not one person there seemed to recognize Danni. Of course, that was because, as Danni had correctly guessed, no one else in the place appeared to be under the age of sixty-five – including the waitresses. The woman in charge of seating people led the girls to a booth in the back. Danni was relieved they weren't sitting near any windows where passers-by could see her, and Sam was thrilled to discover that their booth offered a great view of all the other tables, so she could see what everyone was eating.

"Danni," she whispered, "look at the size of that

man's sandwich! It's as big as his whole head! How does he expect to eat it?"

Danni quietly chided her little sister. "Will you chill? Don't go eyeballing other people's..." She caught sight of the massive amount of meat between the two slices of bread. "Wow! If he eats the whole thing, he'll need to be wheeled out of here!"

Sam picked up the menu. It was huge. She studied it carefully. "What's a 'nosh'?" she asked.

Danni shrugged. "No idea."

Running her finger down the left side of the menu, Sam found many unfamiliar things. "What about a 'latke'? Or 'kugel'? What's this 'knish' thingy?"

"Yo!" Danni grabbed the menu out of Sam's hands. "I don't know any of these weird foods. Here." She pointed. "They have hot dogs. You know what those are, don't you?"

Sam stuck out her tongue at her sister as she took back her menu. "Just because you're too chicken to try new stuff, doesn't mean I have to be."

Danni held her menu up to hide her face from the other customers as she stuck out her tongue back at Sam. The girls started goofing around so much that they didn't notice the waitress arrive at their table.

"What can I get you ladies today?" she asked.

"We aren't exactly sure," Sam replied. "Could you please tell us what all these are?"

The waitress didn't understand. "All these *what?*"

"All these foods!" Sam pointed up and down the menu.

"The whole menu?" the waitress exclaimed. "Are you kidding me? I have twelve tables to serve. Look for something you already know, like a hot dog."

Sam felt a tap on her shoulder. She turned to find herself nose-to-nose with a kind-faced elderly woman from the next table.

"Don't let Ms. Grumpy there stop you from enjoying your lunch," said the woman. "I'm Pauline. I've been coming here since the place opened and it would be my pleasure to explain the menu to you."

Pauline told the waitress to come back in five minutes; in that time she gave Sam and Danni a crash course on deli foods, from borscht to tsimmes. By the time the waitress returned, Sam was ready.

"We'll start with matzo-ball soup for me and kreplach soup for my sister," she said confidently.

"Then we'll have two corned-beef sandwiches on rye bread, along with a nosh of chopped liver, an order of latkes with apple sauce, a plate of blintzes, some gefilte fish and a kugel."

Pauline burst into applause. Danni joined in. Sam blushed.

Knowing there was no way the two girls were ever going to be able to eat all that food, the waitress asked mockingly, "Will that be all?"

"Oh, no!" Sam answered genuinely. "For dessert, we'd like one baked apple, one black and white cookie, and some halva."

The food came quickly – and there was a ton of it! Two huge bowls of soup and plates piled high with meat and noodles. Every square centimetre of the tabletop was covered.

Danni let out a huge groan. "This is so embarrassing. We've ordered far too much. If anybody saw me right now, they'd guess I have a raging over-eating disorder!"

With her mouth full of the best sandwich she'd ever tasted, Sam happily replied, "No worries. We'll take the leftovers home to Mom. She'll love this!"

Sam found every item delicious, except for the gefilte fish – which made her gag – and the halva – which felt like dried paste in her mouth. When the waitress asked if everything was fine, Sam replied, "Fine? I've never eaten so much in my entire life! But I'm not sure this halva is good. It tastes kind of stale."

The waitress pulled a fork out of her pocket, stabbed the corner of the halva, tore off a small piece, and popped it into her mouth. She chewed carefully before swallowing.

"Nope," the waitress said seriously, "it's perfect."

The Devine sisters finished stuffing themselves silly. They wobbled out of the restaurant carrying several brown paper bags full of food they'd barely touched. As they stepped into the bright sunshine, Danni fumbled with her bundles as she tried to put on her sunglasses. Meanwhile, Sam noticed a homeless man sitting on the sidewalk with a sign asking for money. She walked over to him.

"I don't have any money, sir," she said, "but we have great leftovers from our lunch if you'd like them."

The man nodded, so Sam set all her food bags on

the ground next to him. He glanced at them and nodded several more times.

He needs this food a lot more than we do, Sam thought as she walked back over to Danni. She took all the bags from her sister's arms.

Danni was so relieved not to be carrying anything for a moment, that it took her a second to realize that along with the food, Sam had grabbed her expensive clutch bag – the one with all her credit cards, cash and keys.

"Hey, Bonehead!" Danni yelled. Sam was setting all the bags down on the ground next to the homeless man. Danni ran over, reached round her sister, and snatched up her clutch bag from the pile of paper bags.

"Maybe the next time you start giving away stuff," she snapped at Sam, "you could make sure it's *yours* to give?"

Sam spent the entire drive home apologizing to Danni. By the time they got home, Danni had chilled out and was back to enjoying the afternoon. She pulled into the driveway, and parked the car. "That was fun, Little Bit." Danni smiled at her sister. "It stinks that we don't get to spend time together like we used to."

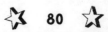

Sam grinned from ear to ear before hopping out of the car and running into the house. Once she reached her room, she plopped herself in front of her computer, and began typing.

Click click click, clack clack click.

Only have a few minutes to write. I need to get over to the stables to meet Olga. Danni and I went out for brunch – just the two of us! It was so nice. Nobody bothered her. She got to be plain old Danni hanging out with plain old me. HEY! Maybe this is the start of something new. Maybe all the rotten things about Danni in all the magazines over the past couple of months, thanks to horrible Harley, have helped Danni see that being famous isn't so great, and maybe, JUST MAYBE, she'll want to stop being a pop star and our family can go back to being normal again! Come on – *it could happen*!

More soon!

Sam hurried outside. She pulled on her favourite smelly cowboy boots, and was busy stomping about to get her feet down deep into the comfy zone, when she was interrupted by a scream from inside the mansion. She ran back into the house.

Sam reached the living room as Rose and Robert, just back from their meeting, did as well. They all found Danni yelling at the television.

"No! That's wrong!" she cried.

Rose put her arms around her daughter. "What's the matter, Honey?"

Danni held up the remote control, hit the rewind button, and after a couple of seconds, hit the play button.

On the TV screen, a promo for the evening's big story on the T2CT daily news broadcast began to play. It showed Sam and Danni entering the deli, while a voice-over hollered, "Danni Devine's nightmare secret!" and then cut to a shaky video of Danni inside the restaurant saying, "I have a raging over-eating disorder."

Rose gasped. She asked how this could have happened, but Danni didn't answer.

"Wait, Mom," she said through tears, "there's more."

The voice-over continued: "Danni is so desperate to

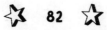

stuff her face, she even steals food!" The video on the TV switched from inside the deli to outside and it showed Danni grabbing her ugly brown clutch bag from the pile next to the homeless man.

Robert shut off the television before pronouncing, "This may *appear* bad, but trust me, I can manage it. Danni –" he pointed at her – "I want you to go and relax. We'll do a press conference later and I need you to look rested and beautiful. Rose –" he nodded her way – "I'm going to have my best people come over and set up a crisis-management phone bank. We'll be taking over the dining room. In the meantime, you and I need to be sure we get our story straight."

"Get what story straight?" Sam shot out. "There's no story! Some creepo taped me and Danni at lunch, and then they cut the video to make it *look* like Danni said and did something awful, but she didn't say or do anything wrong!"

Rose gave Sam a little hug. "I know, Sweetie, I know. This is the harsh part of being famous. *You* didn't do anything wrong. *Danni* didn't do anything wrong. Listen, why don't you go join Olga at the stables and let Robert and me take care of this?"

"But I can help, Mom! I can totally fix this!" Sam reached for the phone. "I was there! We can call a bunch of reporters and I'll explain what really happened!"

Robert thrust out his hand. "Don't touch that!"

Sam picked up the cordless handset. "What, *this*?" She teasingly waved it in the air. "You don't want me to touch *this*?"

Robert's nostrils flared with annoyance. "I need the phone. I have *work* to do."

Sam had a momentary desire to throw the phone at Robert's pearly teeth, but instead she sighed and prepared to toss it to him, when it suddenly rang. Without thinking, she answered it.

"Devine residence," she said, ignoring the horrified expression on Robert's face. "Sure. Hold on, please."

Sam held out the phone. Robert reached for it, but Sam swung her body towards Rose. "It's for you, *Mom*."

Rose snatched the telephone and walked to the other end of the room, listening for a moment before she began speaking in hushed tones. Robert glared at Sam. She responded with her sweetest smile.

When the conversation ended, Rose walked over and slipped herself down onto the sofa.

"Girls," she whispered. "It looks like we might have something else to deal with right now. Come here and sit on the sofa with me."

Sam and Danni did as requested. Rose hugged her daughters as she spoke. "That was the International Red Cross calling back. They believe they have a possible link to your father's family. They warned me not to get too—"

Before Rose could finish, Sam had jumped to her feet. "*Yes!*" She was so excited she began to dance around the living room. "We've got people! We've got family! We've got an ancestor!"

Rose reached out to calm Sam. "Honey, the first thing the Red Cross warned against was getting too excited."

"Hang on," Robert interjected. "Little Miss Squirt here hooks into the Red Cross *last night* and they find some long-lost relative *today*? I don't buy it."

Sam rolled her eyes in annoyance. "It's called *technology*, Robert. It's pretty fast. You should try it some time."

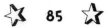

Rose stepped between the two of them. "I asked the same thing, Robert. The woman explained that their database is rather extensive – so when the information Sam plugged in matched what someone else had already entered, well, they found a potential match."

Crossing his arms, he replied, "This is a set-up. Someone at the data processing place recognized *Rose Devine* as the mother and manager of *Danni Devine* and now they are out to scam you for all your money. It's a classic con. They make movies about this kind of thing."

Rose shot Robert an icy glare. "I do not believe that to be the case here, Robert. How about keeping your opinions to yourself for the moment, hmm?"

Sam was beside herself with excitement; she had a long-lost relative *and* her mom was putting Robert in his place. This day *couldn't* get any better!

"So, Mom," Danni said softly. "Who do they think they've found? Some cousin? An aunt or an uncle?"

"They wouldn't say," Rose answered in an equally gentle tone. "Apparently whoever it is is rather old, so they want to make sure the person is still in good health before they try and arrange for us to speak or meet."

Robert clapped his hands. "Good. Then it's settled – we forget about this for now and go back to dealing with Danni's public relations..." He searched for the best word. "...setback."

"What do you mean?" Sam asked in disbelief. "We can't just forget about this – it could be the biggest news of our whole lives!"

"Oh, Sam, chill out, will ya? Did you not see the TV?" Danni pointed at the screen. "Can we please deal with this mess and let the family thing rest? Can you imagine how awful it feels to have everyone in the world think you're a freak?"

Sam sat down next to Danni on the sofa. "Aw, Danni! Nobody thinks you're a freak. That video is a misunderstanding. Like I said, I'll go on the news and explain to everybody what really happened and then it'll all be good again."

"Danni is right to take this afternoon seriously." Robert tried to take control. "Rose, we still need to do crisis control on the press over today's fiasco. This family thing can wait."

Danni tried to tell Sam to hush at the same moment as Sam began to argue with Robert about sticking his nose in personal family business. It got rather loud and unpleasant in the room, until Rose stuck two fingers in her mouth and let out a loud, piercing whistle.

"Enough! No more talking!" Rose yelled. Once the room was quiet, she continued softly. "Robert and I have to focus on fixing this lunchtime public relations disaster before we even begin to go any further with this new family situation. I suggest Danni and Sam, you both go to your bedrooms and—"

"But *Mom*!" Sam whined. "Olga is waiting for me at the stables!"

Rose closed her eyes, took in a lungful of air and slowly exhaled. "Please don't interrupt, Samantha Sue," she said in a spookily calm voice. "Just be home for dinner, okay?"

"Okay." Sam walked to the edge of the living room.

"Oh, Little Bit?" Rose's voice sang out.

"Yes, Mom?"

Rose walked over and leaned in so that she and Sam were forehead to forehead. "Two little things before you take off, Sweetie. Number one: whatever you do, please do not breathe a word to anyone about this family thing. All right?"

Sam nodded.

"Good," Rose continued in a loving voice. "Number two: if those stinky cowboy boots are ever inside this house again, I will go through the family photo album, find a snapshot of you as a bare-bottomed baby, and have it posted on the biggest billboard in town. Do we have an understanding?"

Sam nodded.

Rose gently tapped her daughter on the nose. "Good. Go."

Feeling as though she'd escaped certain doom, Sam ran out the back door. She grabbed her bike from the garage and pedalled at warp speed over to the SuAn Stables.

CHAPTER 7

When she reached the stop sign down the street from the stables, Sam took a moment to catch her breath and pulled out her cellphone to check the time.

"Only a couple of minutes behind schedule," she said. "Maybe I'll get lucky and Olga will be running late too."

As she put her head up and reached for the handlebars, she noticed a car had pulled up next to her. Without bothering to look over, she waited for the car to drive off, but it didn't. It just sat there.

Slowly, Sam turned her head to see why the car wasn't moving. When she realized that it was the Jeep

carrying the camera crew, she let out a groan.

"Come on, you guys," Sam moaned, "not now! Please? Give me a break! Haven't I already had enough of your video camera-related trauma for one day?"

Michi kept her eye to the camera and continued filming as she spoke. "You are *not* hinting that you think *we* had anything to do with that video of you and your sister today, are you?" she asked. "Because Lou and I are professionals! We do our best to stay out of the way and we'd never compromise our work by selling it to some cheap tabloid! That tape was amateur! It—"

Michi suddenly froze. Then she nodded. Her free hand went to her ear; she nodded again, and let out a sigh. She pulled out her earpiece and handed it to Sam.

"Blu wants to talk to you," she said.

A perplexed Sam held the earpiece to her head. "Yes?"

Blu's voice poured into her brain. "You know that neither Michi, nor Lou, nor I had anything to do with what happened today at the deli?"

Sam nodded into the camera.

Blu continued, "Good. Then do me a favour and apologize to Michi."

Looking directly into the lens, Sam whispered, "I'm sorry for what I said, Michi."

Still filming, Michi gave Sam a big thumbs up.

Sam looked away, but thought of something else and quickly looked back into the camera lens.

"Blu!" she yelled. "Blu! You still there?"

"Ouch! Yes, I'm still here. Could you please work on your volume?"

"Sorry! My bad," Sam whispered. "Anyway, you saw the whole thing with the Red Cross calling to say they think they found some relative of my dad's, yeah?"

"Yes," Blu responded.

Sam's voice got louder as her enthusiasm began to take over again. "Isn't that amazing? I can't wait to tell Olga!"

"Sam!" Blu shouted. "Hush yourself, girl! Didn't what happened to Danni at lunch today teach you anything? You shouldn't be speaking about this in public! You never know when some yo-yo with a cellphone is going to grab a snippet of you saying something completely innocent and sell it to make money at your expense!"

Cringing, Sam looked around to see if anyone was peering at her through the bushes. She knew Blu was right, but it was so hard to pretend nothing was going on when she was so excited.

"And another thing you need to consider, *if* you ever do meet up with this long-lost relative…" Blu's voice was much softer now. "He or she may not want to get all close, warm and fuzzy with you."

"What does *that* mean?" she asked.

"Sam, *you* have problems dealing with the wackiness of fame, and you've had a whole *year* to figure out how to deal with it. Imagine how strange it could be for someone new to your world. A private person may not want all the craziness that comes along with your sister and her TV show."

Sam was speechless. She hadn't even considered her long-lost relative *not* wanting to be involved with her.

"Hey." Blu's voice brought Sam back to the moment. "I can see Olga through one of my long-range cameras. Her horse is already saddled; she's waiting for you."

Without speaking, Sam handed Michi back her

earpiece. She rode her bike through the stables' entrance and past the little guard shack without stopping. She didn't even blink as the stable's manager, Mr. Wattabee, ran out and yelled at her – *again* – for not following the rules about signing in. Sam kept pedalling; she knew that Lou and Michi would be right behind her and that would be enough to get Mr. W off her back. It still drove Sam crazy how Mr. Wattabee was so desperate to be an actor that he'd pretend to be nice to her if the cameras were around, when in truth, he was a grumpy man with no sense of humour. Sure enough, when the video crew pulled up at the rail and honked to be let in, Mr. Wattabee growled that it was not his job to raise the security bar, until he saw who was doing the honking.

"No problem, Samantha," Mr. W hollered, even though she was already inside the stables. He didn't care; he was busy making sure the camera was getting his good side. "I'll sign you in. My pleasure. Happy to help."

He would have kept on talking if Lou hadn't yelled, "Buddy, could you just let us in?"

By this time Sam was getting off her bike on the

other side of the stables. She leaned it against a wall and walked over to where Olga was standing with Thunder Bay completely saddled and ready to go.

"Thanks, Olga," Sam said gratefully. "I *so* need this."

"You and me both," replied her friend. "My mom's doing some photo shoot in our backyard and Inga was *such* an obnoxious brat that Mom ordered *both* of us out of the house. Inga's spent the last hour following me around, driving me crazy, until those goofy girls she hangs with – that so-called 'fashion club' – finally showed up. Watch yourself – they're looking for the next victim of one of their –" Olga shuddered – "*fashion makeovers.*"

Sam gave an understanding little snort as she walked her horse over to the gate that led to the freedom of the stable's hills and trails. While waiting for Olga to fetch her own horse and join her, Sam spotted the Jeep with the camera crew heading towards her.

Unfortunately, Sam wasn't the only person to see Michi and Lou. From the other side of the stables, Inga had noticed them as well. She ran over as fast as her pink, high-heeled cowboy boots would let her. Once

she reached the gate, Inga turned her back on Sam so she could face the camera by the time the Jeep was within filming range.

"Gracious," Inga said sarcastically. "What do we have here? Miss Sam Devine hanging out all by her lonesome? That's *way* sad."

Sam was so surprised by Inga's snarky tone that she stared at her in silence.

'What's the matter?" Inga asked mockingly. "Were none of *my* relatives free today, or did they get enough of you last night? That's right, I know how you invited *all my cousins* to your house, but not *me*. And I know my cousins found some important box with a really old picture in it."

Sam's stomach did a nasty flip. "Inga," she begged. "Please keep your voice down."

Olga hurried over to Sam's side. "Hush, Inga! You've got no one to blame but yourself and your big mouth for me not bringing you last night."

At this point, Inga's fashion-club friends caught up and gathered around her. "You think you're awesome because your sister is famous," she snarled at Sam, "but Danni Devine is *way yesterday*! We don't like her

any more." Inga's entourage nodded in unison. "We only listen to Harley now! *She's* not a big, second-rate phoney."

Sam felt her temperature rise. "What do you mean *phoney?*" she asked.

Inga laughed. "Are you, like, the last person on Earth to know what *everyone* is saying? How uncool Danni is, how she doesn't even write her own songs!"

"Inga," Sam said quietly, "Danni never claimed to be a songwriter. She's a singer, pure and simple. You want to talk phoney? *Yesterday* you claimed to be Danni's number one fan, and today you're all into Harley? Talk about *uncool.*" Sam tried to escape the horrible moment. She began to lead Thunder Bay around Inga and into the field. Unfortunately, as she swung the horse round, he raised his tail and pushed out a stinky load of horse poop that landed right on Inga's brand-new boots!

The next two minutes were a blur. Inga screamed, Sam shouted, and everybody at the stables heard every word.

* * *

Click click click, clack clack click.

I messed up on a global scale. In the twenty minutes I was away from home this afternoon, I managed to do EXACTLY what my mom asked me not to.

Here's the quick scoopage: *we think we've found a long-lost relative!* Mom told me to keep this a secret, but at the stables, Inga got me so upset that I lost my temper and hollered at the top of my lungs that me, my sister, my mom, and my *long-lost whoever* are none of her business! I can't believe I allowed Inga to get me that upset. I should know better.

But wait, there's more. (sigh)

As I'm making a fool of myself, yelling like a loser, I notice a bunch of people watching my horrible behaviour. I guess somebody in the crowd used their phone to record Danni Devine's little sister throwing a temper tantrum in public,

because in the brief amount of time it took for me to hand Thunder Bay over to Olga and ride my bike home, our driveway managed to get totally blocked by photographers and paparazzi all screaming for Danni to come out of the house and comment on her crazy little sister and the new rumour about her *long-lost relative*.

Finally, I get inside the house and it's disaster central! Every phone is ringing, Mom is talking into two headsets, and Robert is barking into his silly wrist-phone. But then I see Danni sitting alone at the top of the stairs, looking sad.

It was too much; I had to confess. When I did, Danni said nothing was my fault, the situation was what it was because she was famous, and that it was her who should be apologizing to me for making my life so darn complicated!

So, Danni and I are having this awesome sisterly time—

Rose's piercing voice suddenly came zinging out of the intercom, surprising Sam so much that she jumped and slammed her knee against the bottom of her desk – again.

"Calling Samantha. Calling Danni. This is your mother speaking. I need you both to meet me in the kitchen, *now*. Repeat, meet me in the kitchen, *immediately*."

The two sisters left their bedrooms and hurried down to the kitchen where they found their mom leaning on the centre kitchen island, staring deeply into the countertop. Robert was next to her, intently reading and rereading a piece of paper.

"Mom?" Danni asked. "Robert? What's up?"

Rose slowly looked up at her daughters and drew in a breath before explaining, "I can't believe I'm saying this, but according to the International Red Cross, your grandfather, Mr. Abraham Zabinski, is still alive."

Danni's jaw dropped so hard it almost hit the floor. She was stunned silent. Sam, on the other hand, began shrieking with joy and bouncing around the kitchen.

"This is the best news *ever*!" She elbowed Danni in the side. "Admit it, admit this is the best news ever.

Our grandpa! Our dad's dad! This is so beyond any good thing that has ever happened to me – ever!"

"How is this possible, Mom?" Danni scratched her head. "Wouldn't our grandfather be, like, a hundred years old?"

"I was thinking the same thing," Robert chimed in. "This whole affair doesn't seem right."

Rose ignored Robert. "The Red Cross people say he is seventy-six years old, but still fit and healthy and he would like to meet us."

Sam, still bouncing around, hopped over to Rose. "Where is he, Mom? Where does our grandpa live? When can we see him?"

"We can't go now, Sam," Rose gently explained. "Your grandfather lives in a small town in England."

"England?" Sam stopped bouncing for a second, but then continued with even more gusto. "England! That's so awesome!"

"England?" Danni asked. "You mean like out in the East, those states like Vermont and Maine?"

"No, Honey," Rose gently corrected her. "You're thinking of *New* England. Your grandpa lives in *old* England...the *real* England...the country."

"The land of Shakespeare and castles and kings and queens!" Sam added enthusiastically.

Danni appeared deep in thought. "Hey, isn't that where they had the machine that chopped off people's heads?"

"No." Sam laughed. "You're thinking of France. They had the guillotine."

"Hmm, that's too bad," Danni said.

Everyone stared at her as if she'd lost her mind. When she looked up and saw this, Danni let out a giggle and explained, "I was just dreaming; if we were going to end up travelling all the way over to England to meet our grandpa *anyway*, and it *was* the place with the head-chopper thingy, then I might have taken advantage of the situation and invited Harley along – you know, in a show of being super-mature and above all her nastiness. Then I thought, terrible accidents can happen when people are on vacation, you know – people slip, they fall, they end up with their head in a chopper-thingy." She sighed playfully and turned to Robert. "We can't get one of those machines over here, can we?"

Robert smiled and seemed about to respond, but instead he froze.

"Robert?" Danni asked. "You okay?"

Suddenly Robert snapped back to attention. "Here! I'm here! Yes, Danni." He smiled his huge white grin. "That was funny."

Uh-oh, Sam thought. *He's up to something. He's just come up with some hare-brained scheme that's going to end up messing with my life again.* Before Sam could say anything, Robert had turned his full attention on her mom.

"Listen, Rose," he said, way too earnestly, "I've been thinking that you and the girls deserve a little quiet family time. Things with Danni's career have gotten out of hand, and now with the press digging about to discover who the long-lost relative is…" He glared at Sam. "Nice job keeping *that* quiet." He returned to Rose. "…I think the best thing would be for you and the girls to spend four days at a retreat, a spa – somewhere quiet and secluded. I know the perfect place. It's in the mountains, and there are no telephones, televisions or computers. You'll have time to reconnect and de-stress while I take care of things here."

Rose began to argue with him, but he cut her off. "Please, let me handle everything with the grandfather

situation. I can keep it discreet. I'll make contact with him and arrange for the best way for you to meet face-to-face. If you think about it, this makes the most sense – you see, I can keep it off the paparazzi's radar and we won't scare off the old man." Robert dramatically set his hands on top of Rose's. "Please, let me do this. Allow me to take care of you at this crazy emotional time."

Sam seriously thought she was going to hurl. Robert was oh-so-obviously up to no good. She waited for her mom to call him on it, but Rose didn't. Instead she smiled and thanked him for taking such great care of her little family!

"Mom…" Sam struggled not to burst into tears. "You are *not* going to let Robert make all kinds of plans for us, are you?" Seeing Rose look away, Sam knew she'd already lost this battle, but she begged anyway. "Please, Mom! I don't want to go to a retreat! It sounds horrible! No TV? No computer? No phone?"

Rose hugged Sam. "And that's exactly *why* I think this is an outstanding idea. A little time to ourselves, with no distractions. Robert, make the plans. Girls, pack your bags!"

 104

I have NO time to finish this blog!! I was telling you about the great time I had with my sister, but now Mom, Danni and I have been tricked (yes – TRICKED) into going away for a couple of days to a place with NO COMPUTERS! Robert set this up and I just know it's going to turn out to be a total disaster. (sigh)

Wait!!! NEWS!!! The long-lost relative??? It's my GRANDFATHER!! My dad's dad – the guy in the picture, Abraham Zabinski!!! Robert's arranging for us to meet him when we get back from this four-day jail...I mean retreat (no, I mean JAIL)!! This is the biggest thing in my whole life and I don't have time to blog about it. This is SO BEYOND unfair!!!

MSS (More Super-Soon)!

Sam posted her blog before standing up and stretching. A moment later, her mom pounded on her door and called out, "Young lady, when I return in

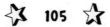

sixty seconds, that light will be off and your body will be in bed!"

Sam raced over to the giant mirror and tapped on it to get Blu's attention.

"Blu," she whispered loudly. "Blu! I've only got a few seconds! Blu? You in there?"

A lazy yawn filled the room.

"Of course I'm here," came the groggy response out of the hidden speakers around the bedroom. "As long as we're taping, I have no life. You know that. What do you want?"

Sam smiled sweetly. "I simply want to say goodbye before our spa trip."

"That's sweet, but I won't be missing you too much."

"Hey," Sam cried. "That's not nice. Why would you say that?"

"Because you can't *miss* somebody when you're still going to be seeing them every day."

"Huh?"

"The crew will be travelling with you, which means, for all practical purposes, I'll be right there with you too, every step of the way. If you were going further away – let's say, crossing time zones – then I'd travel

along in person, but for something like this, I can watch everything from right here."

Once Blu's words sank in, an embarrassed Sam giggled. The very next moment, Rose opened the bedroom door, reached her hand in, shut off the light, and yelled out a final, "Goodnight, Samantha."

Standing alone in the middle of her dark bedroom, Sam felt silly.

"Blu?" she softly called out.

"Goodnight, Samantha," Blu answered, mimicking Rose's serious tone.

Sam giggled once more, jumped into bed and was asleep before her head hit the pillow.

CHAPTER 8

Click click click, clack clack click.

FINALLY! Four days with no screens (TV, cellphone, computer) was a *nightmare*. Every second I kept thinking of stuff I wanted to share with Olga or you – my readers. Michi was a total sport about letting me borrow her earpiece to talk to Blu, but I think I did it too many times and he got annoyed with me – SORRY, BLU!!!

So – I have news!!! I'm not typing this from my bedroom – nope. I'm in an airport, waiting for an

aeroplane that will take me, Mom, Danni, Robert (yeuch), Michi, Lou and OLGA (!!!!!) over to LONDON, ENGLAND!!!

Today, we got picked up at the prison (okay, okay – *retreat*) by Robert, who explained that ABRAHAM ZABINSKI HAD AGREED TO MEET WITH US AS SOON AS POSSIBLE! Robert actually arranged everything! He had suitcases packed for us and had bought our tickets and plotted out our whole schedule.

Mom was a little uneasy at first, until Robert mentioned the name of our hotel in London. I guess it's super-fancy and all kinds of famous people stay there (that makes sense since Danni is world-famous too – I still forget that sometimes – LOL). Robert says he's covered all the details to make sure the paparazzi don't know about our trip, and that our retreat (blah) gave him the opportunity to handle some major career stuff for Danni – so we should all relax and enjoy the trip. But I have a funny feeling that there's more to this, so my eyes and ears are wide open.

Here's the plan: we'll be over in London for a three-day visit with our grandpa and then we'll return home on a huge ship so we can have another four quiet days of Mom, Danni and Sam — "together" time. I was going to challenge Robert about why we needed even more family time (I love my family, but we've just had four days with nothing to do but hike and talk — I'm covered in the quality time department for a while).

Okay, here's where you can see how much I've grown up since last year. Like I said, I knew something was funky with this whole sudden trip across the planet, so I thought at least I could start asking Robert questions about why *he* was coming along on our *family* trip. He could tell I wasn't going to stop bugging him, so guess what he did to get me to hush?

He told me I could bring OLGA!

Yup – I may not be a teenager yet, but I know a good bribe when I see one, and I took it! Robert convinced Mom it would be good for me to have my best friend along for support, Mom called Mrs. V, and Mrs. V agreed. Olga is on her way to meet me here at the airport *right now*!!!

I'm going to London! I'm going to London with my mom, my sister, my best friend and my other best friend (Michi told me that Blu is already there setting things up) and we are going to meet a grandpa that I never knew existed! I have to write this all in a book someday because this is so beyond ANYTHING!

I'm going to London! I'm going to meet my grandfather!!! Oh...should I call him Mr. Zabinski? Would it be better to call him *Grandpa* or *Granddad* or *Grandfather*?

More soon!!!

* * *

"Mom," Sam groaned, "I really have to go to the bathroom! How long till they turn off the seat belt sign?"

Rose looked across the aisle at her daughter. "Sweetie," she cooed, "you've flown before. You know you have to wait until the plane is level."

Sam clenched her teeth and snorted in displeasure.

Olga pulled out a stack of magazines from her travel bag. "Hey, Sam. I brought these for us. Trick your mind into forgetting you have to go and you'll be fine."

"It's not my *mind* I'm worried about," Sam grumbled. Three seconds later she howled, "I'm dying over here! How can they torture people like this? We've been flying for what, one, two hours?"

From the seat behind her came Robert's snarky voice: "Fifteen minutes. Fifteen long, loud, obnoxious minutes."

Sam and Olga both launched into wicked giggle fits.

After the pilot announced that she was turning off the fasten seat belt sign, and Sam got to run to the bathroom, the two friends dug into Olga's magazines. They made fun of all the wild clothes and crazy hairdos on the fashion models.

Hearing the giggles, Danni popped up from her seat in front of Sam and Olga.

"Anything interesting in that pile, there?" she asked.

"Not completely sure," Olga answered. "My mom saw this as an opportunity to clean off her coffee table and dumped all this in my carry-on. I have no idea what's here."

Danni grabbed the top magazine. "Let's see." She studied it carefully. "This sounds interesting." She read the cover out loud. "'Harley – *the* interview – on keeping it real and snagging the title of pop's *Devine* princess'." She handed back the magazine. "I'll pass."

Olga tried to apologize but Danni cut her off. "No worries. Harley is everywhere. I see her face on every TV, every magazine, every billboard. There's no escape."

Before Sam or Olga could think of a response, Danni walked around to stand next to Robert. He was so focused on reading some very legal-type papers that he didn't notice her. She looked down at the pile of papers in the seat next to him and saw her name.

"So, what fabulous career move are you planning for me now, Robert?" she asked wearily.

It was rare that anything flustered big-shot music agent Robert Ruebens, but Danni had surprised him and he jumped, reaching out to quickly gather all his papers.

"Danni." Robert ran a hand through his hair and tried to appear completely cool and in control. "There are several interesting opportunities, but nothing worth discussing yet. Let me deal with the business of your career. Why don't you sit down and watch a movie?"

Robert turned his attention back to his papers. Danni shuffled back to her seat, but before she got there, a pretty flight attendant tapped her on the shoulder.

"I am sorry to bother you, Miss Devine," she said kindly. "I realize this is an unusual request, but we have a young girl travelling by herself and she's been crying since her mother put her on the plane. The only time she stopped was when she overheard the other passengers talking about you being on-board. Would you mind popping to the back of the aircraft with me to say hello to her?"

Danni almost refused; she was in no mood to cheer up anyone. However, the idea that she could really help a sad kid made her think twice. She told the flight attendant to lead the way.

Walking to the back of the plane, Danni immediately spotted the girl. Her face was all red and puffy from crying. Danni slipped into the aisle seat next to her.

"Howdy," she chirped. "Mind if I sit here a minute?"

When the little girl saw who was next to her, her mood amped. She wiped her eyes on her sweater and sat up straight to appear grown-up and mature.

Danni held out her hand. "I'm Danni Devine. What's your name?"

"I'm Rowan Brown. I'm ten. I think you're awesome! I'm a big fan, maybe your biggest! Getting to meet you is the best thing that's ever happened to me!"

Rowan's glee raised Danni's spirits.

"Want to watch the movie with me?" Rowan grinned from ear-to-ear. "I have an extra set of headphones *and* an extra bag of pretzels!"

Danni couldn't refuse; both girls settled in to enjoy the in-flight entertainment. After a couple of movie previews, the next thing to come up on the screen was a showbiz report entitled "Hot or Not". On the left side of the screen was the word "Hot" and a picture of

Harley. Across from that, on the right, was the word "Not", and a picture of Danni.

Rowan pulled off her headphones. "That's baloney! Your real fans don't believe any of that junk! Harley is nothing but a bully!"

Danni was too touched to speak. She smiled gingerly and nodded. Suddenly the plane began bouncing around in the sky. The pilot's voice came over the loudspeaker; she wanted everyone to fasten their seat belts. The pretty flight attendant hurried over to help Danni back to her proper seat.

"Rowan," Danni said, as she pulled out a business card, "it was a total pleasure getting to hang with you. This is my e-mail address. I'd love to hear from you some time."

Rowan's enormous smile sent Danni back to her seat with a wonderful, warm feeling. Olga was snoozing away by now, but Sam was still awake to notice Danni's great mood as she strode past to reach her seat.

"What are you so happy about?" Sam asked. "Where have you been?"

"Nowhere," came the reply. "Just hanging with a buddy."

Sam didn't understand, but seeing as her big sister was in such a good mood, she was cool. She reached into her bag, grabbed her camera, and called out, "Say cheese!"

Danni beamed. "Cheese!"

Unfortunately, as Sam was taking the photo, the plane bumped again; Sam ended up with a shot of her sister falling over.

"Danni?" Sam cried out.

"I'm fine," she answered, picking herself up. "What is it you say? Nothing bruised but my big old ego."

Danni was still feeling so great that she giggled as she climbed into her seat. Then she snuggled into a blanket, fastened her seat belt, and fell right off to sleep.

Sam pondered on Danni's odd behaviour for a moment, toying with the idea of blogging what had just happened. But one second after the thought entered her head, she too was drifting into dreamland.

CHAPTER 9

Despite the nap, the long flight and change in time zones zapped Sam's energy. She shuffled off the plane, through passport control, and struggled to keep her eyes open while standing around with everyone as they waited for their bags at the luggage reclaim.

When all their stuff had arrived, Sam followed along as Robert led the group towards the exit. One minute, everything was mellow, but the second Robert pushed open the security doors separating the arrivals section from the rest of the airport, everything immediately went off-the-charts insane! Ear-splitting levels of yelling and squealing, blinding flashes of light, and a sea of people all descended upon the Devines.

"Grab hands!" Robert shouted. "I'll push us through."

Sam was afraid of getting squished by the crowd that was desperately trying to get to Danni; it was almost impossible to breathe. Once they managed to get through all the people and climb into their waiting limo, they were forced to sit at the kerb until the police had moved everyone out of the way.

When the limousine finally did get out of the airport, Sam glanced about to see if anyone else was weirded out by what had just happened. Danni's hand was shaking as she applied her favourite lipgloss, but otherwise everybody seemed okay. When Sam looked up towards the front of the limo, she found herself nose-to-lens with Michi and her trusty video camera.

She chuckled at the insanity of it all – flying around the planet, getting mobbed by fans, and now having their family video crew back, recording their every move.

Then suddenly Sam spied a giant billboard in front of the limo and her mouth dropped open. She was so stunned by it that she couldn't speak; she simply pointed.

Rose was the first to see what had twisted Sam in such knots, and she, too, had a rather strong reaction. Throwing herself across the limo to get a better view, she yelled for the driver to pull over. When he tried to explain that cars are only allowed to do so for emergencies while on the motorway, Rose actually snarled.

"Trust me, Driver, this is about to become one."

The driver pulled over onto the hard shoulder as Rose pushed the button to slide back the sunroof. She stood up through it and glared at the billboard.

Danni was confused. She tugged on Sam's sweater.

"Help me out here, will ya? What's going on?"

Olga moved herself over next to Sam, and pointed upwards. "Look up, Danni," she said. "The sign next to the factory. That billboard has your face on it."

Danni spotted what everyone was talking about. "Oh, wow! Yup, that sure is my face…" She paused. "Hey, is that Harley's face next to mine?" She rubbed her eyes. "Tell me I'm seeing things. Somebody *please* tell me that isn't Harley up there next to me."

There was a long silence.

"Okay, so I guess my face *is* on a billboard with

Harley," Danni muttered. "Great. Sam, read me what it says. I can't look at it again."

Sam swallowed the lump in her throat and began to read. "*Battleship* – the pop event of the year. One night only, a concert of titanic proportions. Join Danni Devine and Harley for their *live* broadcast from the deck of the HMS *Queen Elizabeth 2*. Today's 2 Cool Teens Network presents this once-in-a-lifetime battle for the top pop-star crown!"

Another painfully quiet moment passed before Danni asked, "The *Queen Elizabeth 2*? Isn't that the boat we're taking home next week?"

"The *ship*." Sam immediately regretted correcting her sister. "Yes. That's our boat."

"But…" Danni continued to struggle, "I thought Robert said we were taking the boat home so that we could have a few more days of private family time – peace and quiet. Wasn't that the plan?"

Rose, still standing with her head outside the sunroof, yelled down, "Yes, Danni. That *was* the plan that was explained to us by *Mr. Ruebens*."

Sam, Olga and Danni all slowly turned to glare at Robert. He straightened his tie before speaking.

"Excuse me, ladies," he said. "I believe I am wanted up top."

Robert stood and joined Rose. At first, Rose and Robert spoke only in hushed tones, but that didn't last. Soon, Rose was yelling. The pitch of her voice got higher and higher as she peppered Robert with questions as to how he'd managed to turn a family vacation into an international event with Danni's nemesis, seemingly overnight. She called him a liar, a louse, and a giant turkey. Sam almost laughed out loud at that last one, but she had the good sense to slam her hands over her mouth to stifle herself.

When Rose asked Robert when he'd planned on telling Danni that she was going to perform with the *very girl* who'd been ripping Danni apart in the press, Robert actually stammered. He said something about the whole crossing being a huge ego boost for Danni, seeing as she'd be surrounded by so many fans.

Immediately, Rose's voice changed from high and screechy to low and spooky. She demanded that Robert explain *exactly* what he meant by "surrounded by so many fans". He gulped before admitting that the T2CT Network was running an online contest and giving away fifty cabins to Harley's fans and another fifty to Danni's fans (fans meaning the actual contest winner and a parent) as a way to build an immediate, global buzz for the concert. This once-in-a-lifetime chance for fans to get to spend four fabulous days at sea with their favourite pop singer, either Danni or Harley, had already, in just the past ten hours since the contest went live on the web, begun generating the kind of positive publicity for Danni that he and Rose had been trying to drum up for the past three months!

"A *schmooze cruise*!?!" shrieked Rose. "You booked my family on a cheap, tacky *schmooze cruise*?"

"What's a shoes cruise?" Sam asked Olga.

"Not shoes," Olga whispered, "*schmooze*. Schmooze means friendly chat, like when you hang with your friends, you gab, you talk, you goof; that's schmoozing."

"Hold on." Danni leaned forward and twirled a strand of hair around her fingers furiously, the way she always did when she was thinking hard. "So…Robert lied to us – totally, completely *lied* to us? Instead of putting us on the boat so we could have time away from cameras and crowds, he invited the whole world to come and hang out with us?"

"And Harley," Sam growled.

Danni sat back in her seat and covered her face with her hands.

Sam reached out to comfort her sister, but as she did, her mother's voice rang out loud and clear.

"We are done, Robert! D-O-N-E – *done*! The minute we reach our hotel, you will cancel the concert and begin the paperwork to sever all business ties between your-sorry-self and my family."

Robert tried to charm his way out of trouble, but Rose cut him off.

"The last thing you will do for us will be to assist and escort myself, Danni, Sam and Olga for the duration of this trip, because I am sorely out of my element and I stupidly allowed you to make all the travel plans. Do I make myself clear?"

Sam didn't hear an answer, so she guessed that Robert must have nodded.

"Good! Fine! Discussion over!" Rose barked. "All I care about is making sure my daughters get to meet their long-lost grandfather and that we return home safely and put all of this, and *you*, behind us for good!"

With that, Rose dropped back down into her seat

and ordered the limo driver to get moving. He did, hitting the accelerator so hard that the limo lurched forward and Robert almost flew out of the sunroof.

The rest of the drive into the city was tense. No one dared to speak.

Even though Sam knew that Robert was a total creep who deserved all this trouble, she couldn't help but notice how truly wretched he looked. If she hadn't known better, she might have believed he was feeling bad about what he had done – but then, she *did* know better. She turned her head towards the window and tried not to think about him.

"Excuse me, sir," Sam politely asked the limo driver, "how much longer till we get to our hotel?"

"Traffic isn't too bad this time of day, Miss. I expect to have you there in about half an hour," he replied.

Sam sighed; only a few minutes ago she would have killed for a nap, and now, when she had the perfect opportunity, she was so wound up she couldn't imagine having to sit still for another second, let alone an excruciating thirty minutes.

They left the motorway and began to wind their way through the streets of London. Sam was impressed

with the way the driver managed to manoeuvre the long limo through the crowded and sometimes frighteningly narrow streets, plus she was tripped out by the whole cars-driving-on-the-opposite-side-of-the-street-from-back-home thing. She was so busy focusing on the traffic that she didn't notice they had pulled up outside a beautiful old building, but once the driver ran round to open the back door, a rush of excitement hit her.

"Are we here, Mom? Are we really here – in *England* – to meet our *grandfather*?"

Even though she was still fuming, Rose had to smile at Sam's enthusiasm.

"That is an affirmative, Little Bit," she replied. "The Devine family has officially arrived in London."

Sam poked her head through the open door and turned back round. "Don't seem to be any paparazzi. Let's go sightseeing!"

Hopping out and taking in a huge breath of chilly London air, Sam turned back to the limo and called out, "Come on! Olga! Danni! Get out here!"

The bummer for Sam was that *her* yelling for her sister alerted the hiding photographers to Danni

Devine's arrival. The scene changed in an instant. People seemed to pour out of every nearby doorway. Suddenly, the entrance to the hotel was blocked by reporters and cameramen, all snapping pictures or screaming out to Danni for a comment.

The hotel doormen rushed to get Rose, Danni, Sam and Olga past the mob and through the huge wooden hotel doors. As they fought to escape the craziness outside the hotel, Danni glared at Sam.

"Way to go, Slick."

Sam launched into an apology, but stopped when she realized her sister wasn't listening. "Hey." She poked Danni's arm. "I'm talking to you. Why are you ignoring me?"

A distracted Danni replied, "Stop yapping and start looking."

"What?" Sam asked. "Look at wha— *Oh!*"

They were standing in one of the most beautiful places Sam had ever seen. The girl who prided herself on her awesome vocabulary was momentarily too enchanted to speak. The walls around her were covered with beautiful fabrics that made everything appear both comfortable and elegant. Vases overflowed with

flowers. Massive crystal chandeliers sparkled. The people in the lobby seemed effortlessly chic. It was easy for Sam to understand why this hotel was so famous!

"Mom," Sam whispered, "you sure we're allowed in here?"

Rose gave her daughter a loving squeeze. "It is gorgeous, isn't it?"

The spell of the special moment was broken by Robert; he stumbled into the lobby and over to Rose. His hair was messy and his tie needed straightening.

"All right, Rose," he sputtered as he gasped for air, "I got all the luggage onto the bellboy's cart. The hotel manager will be here in a second to give us our keys and show us round the hotel." He glanced at the magnificent lobby. "I'd say I did all right handling the hotel reservations, yes?"

"This appears acceptable," Rose replied coldly as she turned away.

The manager of the hotel, Mr. Walker, came over and introduced himself. Right away, he made Rose, Danni, Sam and Olga feel like honoured guests. As he escorted them, along with Robert, over to the lifts and up to their rooms, he made sure everyone understood

that they had the entire hotel staff at their service.

Sam loved the flat-screen television in the lift. "Mr. Walker," she said, "*that* is one of the coolest things *ever*!" She turned to her mom. "Cancel my room; I'll stay in here!"

Mr. Walker spoke softly to Sam. "Your television is *bigger*."

When they reached the top of the hotel, Mr. Walker reminded everyone that this was a *private* floor – the lift would only go this far up if a special key was inserted into a hidden slot on the control panel. Should anyone forget or lose their key, they would have to call to be escorted back up. No special key; no access to the floor.

Sam whispered in Olga's ear, "Robert better hold onto his key. I don't think any one of us would let him back up here."

Mr. Walker guided everyone to the first suite and opened the door. He handed Rose a key card and waited as she stepped inside.

"Girls," Rose said, "we all need to rest for a few hours. I want you to go to your rooms, unpack, and nap until I call you for dinner."

Danni rubbed her eyes and yawned. "Sure thing, Mom. I'm half asleep anyway."

"Aw!" Sam whined. "We just got here! I know we can't go see Grandpa yet, but why can't we go exploring?"

"Samantha," Rose replied wearily, "we are in a foreign country. You are only twelve. You are not, under any circumstances, to set foot outside this hotel without adult supervision, and this adult is going to sleep." Rose gave her daughter a kiss on the cheek. "See you in a couple of hours."

Mr. Walker quietly closed the door behind Rose and turned to Danni. She leaned against the wall, pushed some hair out of her face, and let out a massive yawn.

"Stick a fork in me," she said to no one in particular. "This potato is baked."

Sam translated for Mr. Walker: "She means she's really tired and would like the key to her room."

Mr. Walker nodded and went to the door opposite Rose's room. He opened it, handed Danni her key card, and wished her a lovely nap.

"Sam," Danni called out as she was closing her

door, "don't even *think* about calling me to take you outside. I'm *taking* a bath and *taking* a nap – and that's all the *taking* I'm doing for the rest of the day."

Holding out his hand, Robert said, "I'll take my key card as well."

"Very good, sir." Mr. Walker handed a card over and pointed to the far end of the hallway. "Your room is down by the window. Enjoy your stay."

Robert took the key card and shuffled slowly down the hall to his room. For the second time that day, Sam had to remind herself that she absolutely should *not* be feeling sorry for the guy.

"Ladies," Mr. Walker said to Sam and Olga, "your suite is at the other end of this hall. Follow me, please."

"Sure thing—" Something caught Sam's ear. "Did you say *suite*?"

Mr. Walker proceeded to the far end of the floor, placed a key card into the slot on a set of double doors, and swung them wide open. "Here we are."

Sam grabbed Olga's arm. "Our suite! *Our suite!* How rock-star awesome is that?"

Olga grinned from ear to ear. "We have to take pictures and e-mail them to Inga as soon as possible!"

131

The two girls cackled with glee as they followed Mr. Walker into their super-sweet suite! There was a mini-fridge in the living room, right under the colossal flat-screen TV that covered the entire wall directly across from a *most* comfy sofa. The far side of the living room was one giant window and from it they had a perfect view of Buckingham Palace! Mr. Walker pointed out that the cupboards and refrigerator in the full-sized kitchen had been stocked with foods the hotel's staff believed two young ladies would appreciate. Olga walked over and opened a cupboard door.

"Sam!" she exclaimed. "Cookies!"

"In England, we call those biscuits," Mr. Walker explained.

Olga nodded happily. "Okay! Biscuits! Look at all the biscuits! And chips!"

Again, Mr. Walker corrected her. "We call those crisps."

Olga tore into a bag of crisps and began chowing. "I don't care what you call them," she said as she licked the salt from her lips, "these are the yummiest fried potato things ever! Sam, we are in junk-food heaven!"

"Mr. Walker," Sam chimed, "you are a superhero!"

Mr. Walker looked pleased. "We pride ourselves on making our guests feel at home."

Olga laughed. "My kitchen at home *never* feels like this; this is way better!"

Smiling as he moved to leave, Mr. Walker reminded the girls, "if you need anything, don't hesitate to call on me or any of my staff."

"Thank you, sir," Sam called out. She waited until she heard the click of the closed door to dive into the kitchen and tear into her own bag of crisps. "Oh, these smell so good!" She shoved a handful into her mouth. "Wow, they *taste* as good as they smell!"

Sam and Olga spent the next thirty-five minutes eating their way through the kitchen. Their goal was to sample a little of everything, but of course when they tasted something new and found it to be insanely scrumptious, they had to eat it all because it would be a shame to waste anything so tasty.

By the time they'd cleaned out the kitchen and dragged their overly-stuffed selves to the living room sofa, both girls had so much sugar, grease and fat coursing though their veins that they could barely see straight.

"Do you know what my mom would do to me if she ever found out what I just ate?" Olga asked from her position face down on the sofa. "She'd kill me. First, she'd scream, and then she'd kill me." Thinking more about what she'd just said, she rolled onto her side. "They don't have video cameras in here, do they?"

Sam shook her head. "Nah! You saw the camera crew in the limo with us. There's no way they'd have had time to get anything in our rooms so fast."

As Sam remained sprawled on the floor trying to scan for hidden cameras, Olga got up off the sofa and walked to the giant window.

"I can't wait to get out there and see London!" she said wistfully. "It's going to be so unreal to see this world-famous historical stuff up close. People dream their whole lives of coming here, and we made it before the age of thirteen!"

Sam hopped up. "You're right! Let's go!"

Olga whipped round, certain she'd heard incorrectly. "What?"

Sam repeated, "You're right! Let's go!"

"Has the sugar gone to your brain?" Olga asked,

watching in disbelief as Sam struggled to get her shoes on without bothering to untie the laces.

"No, in fact I'm totally *using* my brain," Sam explained. "We came to see my grandpa, but we can't do that until tomorrow. Once we do see him, we'll probably hang at his place, so us going and seeing all there is to see right now is the best idea possible!"

"I guess." Olga nodded hesitantly. "But what do you think your mom is going to do to us if we go outside? Just you and me, toodling around London, with no adult supervision; don't you think we'd be *so* busted?"

An evil smirk spread across Sam's face. She glided over to the telephone. "Olga," she sang as she picked up the receiver, "I have come to learn over the past year that whenever life dumps a truckload of lemons on you, you just have to keep your eyes open for the opportunity to make some lemonade!"

Confused, Olga stared at her friend in bewilderment.

"Trust me," Sam begged before turning her attention to the telephone. She dialled, waited, and then spoke in her most grown-up voice. "Hotel operator?

Hello there. Would you please see if there is a fellow guest by the name of Mr. Malcolm Bluford at this fine hotel? Oh there is? Great! Could you connect me to his room, please?"

CHAPTER 10

The two girls waited anxiously at the reception desk in the hotel lobby, both eager to get out and explore London. Finally, a bell dinged, the lift doors opened, and Michi and Lou came out, with all their video-crew gear. Sam noticed that while Michi looked refreshed and ready to go, Lou was a mess. The poor guy had wrinkles all over his clothes and under his eyes. *Aww, he must have gone into full snooze mode the minute they arrived from the airport*, Sam thought guiltily.

Michi hoisted the camera onto her shoulder. As soon as Sam saw the red "on" light on the video camera, she knew she and Olga were free to escape the hotel. They could explore as much of London as humanly possible within the next hour and a half – by then Rose would be waking up and it would be better for all involved if Sam and Olga were already back in their suite.

The girls ran out of the hotel and over to a bright-red, double-decker, sightseeing bus. They bought tickets, scurried up the stairwell, and were thrilled to find the open top of the bus was entirely empty.

"Cool beans!" Sam exclaimed. "How did we get so lucky?"

Olga pointed up at the threatening grey clouds overhead. "Maybe everybody else knows something we don't."

Sam glanced up, studied the thick, black clouds, and shook her head. "Nah. We're safe. There's *nothing* that's going to ruin our first afternoon in England!"

Olga nodded. "All right, then! So, where will this fine bus be taking us?"

Sam looked Olga straight in the eye. In a very strong, authoritative voice, she told her friend, "I have absolutely no idea."

"What?" Olga exclaimed with a fearful expression.

Sam put her arm around Olga's shoulder. "Relax. I checked on the internet before we left home – these tourist buses only travel around the centre of London. We'll make a big loop and end up right here, in front of our hotel. Trust me – I've got this situation covered."

Olga calmed down. "Okay. I'm good."

Sam and Olga kept running from one side of the bus to the other as they ooh-ed and ah-ed and posed for pictures while the bus drove past some of the most famous sights in the whole world.

When the bus stopped at the end of a long street, the girls jumped off, with Michi and Lou following. They darted over to Buckingham Palace.

Olga was breathless. "I can't believe I'm standing in front of a real, live palace!"

Sam wasn't quite so impressed. "Yeah, it's cool, but where are the horses? This *is* where they do the Changing of the Guard thing, right?"

Olga nodded.

"That's what I thought." Sam was craning her neck, looking all around. "On TV, whenever they show it, there's always a whole bunch of horses. I'm bummed—"

Then out of the corner of her eye, Sam saw a small band of horses coming out of the palace gates. "Look!" She pointed. "Wow! Are those not the most wicked-perfect horses you've ever seen? Man! I *have* to get a picture!"

Sam held up her camera, but was flustered by all the people around her. Each shot she tried to take had some stranger's arm or handbag in it. She tried to lean around one man, but he shifted and ended up elbowing her right in the head. Frustrated, Sam balanced the camera safely on a wall as she looked around for a statue to climb up to try and get above the crowd, but instead she spied Michi pointing to her wristwatch.

"The time! Olga," she cried, "we haven't been watching the time!"

The girls bolted in the direction of their hotel. Luckily, they weren't too far away. As they reached the grand entrance, Sam slowed a bit. "I think we're good," she said looking at her watch. "According to my calculations, my mom should be waking up in about twelve minutes."

Olga nodded and walked through the huge wooden

doors. Sam looked behind her to make sure Lou and Michi were still following – and crashed straight into Olga, who had frozen rock solid the moment she stepped inside the hotel.

"What's the mat—" Sam stopped, because she could see the problem for herself. Standing in the lobby, with her arms crossed and a very displeased scowl upon her face, was a mega-unhappy Rose Devine.

Robert seemed surprisingly upbeat as he raced over to stand next to Olga and Sam. "See, Rose," he chirped, "I told you they'd be fine. There was no need to worry."

Michi and Lou burst through the doors and practically ran over Sam. She knew she was in big trouble, but tried to act as if everything was fine.

"Did you have a nice nap, Mom?" Sam asked.

Without uttering a sound, Rose pointed towards the lift. Sam walked over and hit the "up" button. She grimaced at the irony that her beautiful hotel suite, which had felt like paradise earlier in the day, was now most likely going to become her prison cell.

* * *

Click click click, clack clack click.

Whoa! I'm having the weirdest day of my life.

Let me cut to the chase – I made a kind of stupid move and was on the verge of being in the most trouble of my entire life when – *hold on*, did I mention that we made it to England safe and sound? Well, WE'RE HERE!!!

Let me try again.

I did something that wasn't too smart (but it was FUN) and Mom ordered me (and Olga) into the lift. As we all stepped in (me, Olga, Mom, Robert, Michi and Lou – yeah, it was *crowded*!) the TV in the lift was showing a live entertainment report about a press conference at another hotel in London, and guess who was doing all the talking? HARLEY! *Grrrrrrr!*

Harley was making a big stink about Danni being too chicken to sing on the same stage as her. She was going on and on, spouting off the most rotten things about my big sister. How rude is that?

So there we are, stuffed in a lift, watching this disaster. When we got to our floor, Mom scurried over to Danni's room. She tried to be cool and calm, but Mom was basically pounding on the door. When Danni finally opened up, it was clear she'd been crying. Her eyes were red and her face was puffy. The TV in her living room was still showing Harley's press conference.

Mom and Robert began to argue. She blamed him for putting Danni into such a horrible situation. He shot back that she wouldn't be in the horrible situation if Rose hadn't pulled the plug on the concert. It was awful, but to be honest, part of me was enjoying seeing Mom say the kinds of things to Robert that *I'd* wanted to say for so long.

Then, something amazing happened. Danni cried out, "ENOUGH!" Everybody hushed up fast, as she admitted that there was some truth in the stuff Harley was saying about her being chicken about the concert.

Mom tried to be all comforting, but Danni stopped her and *demanded* that the concert go ahead. She babbled about some kid named Rowan and how she owed it to her real fans to stand up and show Harley and the rest of the world that she is a talent to be reckoned with. Danni ordered Robert to do whatever was necessary to get the gig back on track.

Robert nodded and left the room. And that was that!

Mom wanted all of us to chill out, so she grabbed the room service menu and asked us to order our dinner. I was surprised when Olga said she was so exhausted that all she wanted to do was go back to our room and get some sleep. When Mom got all worried that a lack of appetite might be a sign that Olga was getting sick, I 'fessed up about our major pig-out before leaving the hotel. Instead of giving us a lecture about the dangers of junk food, Mom just rolled her eyes and sighed. She was totally cool! Hey – that's another miracle! Will you look at that? Two miracles in the same evening!

I need to finish up this blog before I fall asleep on top of my computer. Here's how the rest of the night played out:

- Olga went to our suite and got right to sleep.
- Mom, Danni and me had a quiet dinner in Danni's room.
- We talked about meeting our grandpa tomorrow and how awesome and also a little scary it is.
- Mom made us promise not to have any expectations about the meeting and to simply allow whatever will happen to happen – not to try and force any specific thing (like a hug).

Sitting there with Mom and Danni, it was easy to make the promise, but now that I'm alone (well,

not completely alone – Olga is in the other bed), I'm thinking about tomorrow and getting more excited and more nervous. On the one hand, how can I *not* be filled with all kinds of unbelievable excitement at finally getting to meet a member of my dad's family? On the other hand, Abraham Zabinski is a very old man, and he may not care too much about having young granddaughters living on the other side of the planet. Still, on the other hand – wait – that's three hands. Oops! LOL!!!!

That's it – I'm ruined. Time for sleep.

More soon!!!!!

Sam

CHAPTER 11

Sam slept a little, but she was up early the next morning. The thought of getting to meet her father's father had her so wound up that she couldn't concentrate on anything else.

As everyone (Danni, Robert, Olga, Michi and Lou) piled into the limo for the ninety-minute drive out to the little town of Virginia Water, to meet Abraham Zabinski, Rose stopped Sam.

"Honey," she whispered into her daughter's ear, "even though things have gotten all crazy, you must know that I'm very proud of you. Here we are, in the middle of London, going out to meet your grandfather and it's all because of you." Rose gave Sam a kiss on the forehead. "My point is that, while it's usually Danni who gets all the applause, today is *your* day."

Sam totally radiated with pride.

The ride out to Virginia Water was boring until they left the motorway and began driving down the local streets, but Sam didn't notice anything except how slowly the minutes seemed to tick by. After what felt like a billion hours, the limo pulled up outside a little white building with a bright red door.

"Is this the house?" Sam asked excitedly.

"Afraid not," the driver answered. "My satnav seems off. I'm going to run into this post office for better directions."

As the driver disappeared through the red door, Olga turned to Sam. "A post office! Let's get some stamps to take home."

"Good thinking!" Sam nodded.

The girls jumped out of the limo and hurried into the little building. They got inside just as the lady behind the counter scribbled on a scrap of paper.

She handed the paper to the driver. "These directions should get you there in two minutes, but good luck having a conversation with that one. He prefers his own company." She shook her head. "And that ratty old dog, it goes *everywhere* with him."

Sam was stunned. She walked straight back out. Olga raced to catch up with her.

"Don't worry." Olga could see her friend was shaken. "I'm sure your grandpa is a nice man."

Sam didn't answer.

Rose noticed the change in Sam's mood. She reached for her bag. "Little Bit," she said gently, "I brought something to show your grandfather. Maybe you'd like to take charge of it for the moment?"

From her bag, Rose pulled the simple little ring that had been in the box with the photo of Abraham and Golda. It was on a lovely silver chain. Rose hung it around Sam's neck and smiled. "I'm trusting you with something very precious."

The expression on Sam's face was one of total seriousness. "I understand, Mom. Don't worry, I will guard this with my *life*."

Two minutes later, the limo reached Abraham Zabinski's cottage. For someone who'd been so excited earlier, Sam now felt sick with nerves.

Okay, she said to herself. *Remember what Blu told you. He may not want to deal with all the craziness of having famous relatives, but that doesn't mean you can't enjoy chatting with him. Get yourself out of this limo now!*

Sam hopped out of the limousine, and walked past everyone else, straight up to the front door. After taking in a big breath of air and blowing it out, Sam knocked, but then jumped away as fast as she could, spooked by sudden loud barks and growls coming from inside the house. Glancing back, she saw the worried expressions of both Rose and Danni, so she tried to lighten the moment.

"Looks like Mr. Zabinski either has a large dog or a seriously snarky kitty-cat."

From behind her, a voice replied, "I can assure you that Mr. Red here is *all dog*."

Sam crooked her head to see the person connected to the voice. There was an awkward silence as she stared at the small, elderly man standing inside the doorway; he wasn't even close to the picture she'd painted in her mind. This guy was not much taller than she was! His brown eyes were barely visible through his bushy eyebrows, which were in direct contrast to what little grey hair was left on his head. Even though Sam's focus was on the man, she could also see the brownish, blackish, largish mess of dog leaning against him. She was immediately curious as to why a dog who *so* wasn't red would be named *Red*.

Robert stepped forward, but the dog let out another growl.

"*Przestać*, Red," the elderly man ordered as he gently patted the dog's head. "*Przestać*. Be polite. I believe these are the guests we've been expecting."

Robert reached out to shake hands. "Good morning, sir. I am Robert Ruebens; I'm assisting the Devine family. You would be Mr. Zabinski, I presume?"

The elderly gentleman shook Robert's hand and replied, "Yes, you presume correctly. Welcome to my home." He held out his arm. "Please, everyone, come inside. We can share a pot of tea. Come."

Rose, Danni, Sam, Olga, Robert, and the video crew, with all their equipment, followed Mr. Zabinski and Red into the tiny cottage. Sam didn't think there was any way they were going to get all eight people and that big dog into the itty-bitty living room, but somehow, they all squeezed in. Despite what the

woman in the post office had said, Mr. Zabinski seemed to enjoy playing host and helped everyone, even Michi and Lou, find a place to sit.

Robert introduced each person, including the camera crew, to Mr. Zabinski, but no one seemed to know how to get a real conversation going. Sam was afraid that Mr. Zabinski was going to think that they were all rude, or dull as dishwater.

"Mr. Zabinski…" She tried to sound grown-up. "I'm sure it must be bizarro for you to have all of us, and our camera crew, in your house."

The little man shook his head. "Stop, please."

Sam's eyes flew open. She couldn't believe that they'd come all this way and the first time she'd opened her mouth to speak, she'd managed to upset her long-lost grandfather.

"Call me 'Abe'." A twinkle gleamed in his eyes. "*Mr. Zabinski* sounds like an old man, no?"

Realizing her grandfather was both kidding and being kind, Sam was massively relieved. "Mr. Za—" She caught herself. "Sorry. *Abe*. *Abe*, I was guessing that it must be strange for you to have a camera crew videotaping in your home."

Abe shook his head. "No. This, I do all the time."

Sam hadn't expected that. She began to apologize; she hadn't meant to insult her grandfather, but he smiled and waved his hands to get her attention.

"I am joking with you, Samantha," he said as he struggled to get out of his chair. "*Nu*, it was a joke."

That officially broke the tension in the room. Everyone relaxed. Sam rushed over to help Abe get to his feet. He thanked her and for the first time, took a good look at her. It seemed like he recognized something in Sam that made him both happy and sad, but he quickly blinked a couple of times and then turned to speak to the others in the room.

"I am going to make tea now. I have biscuits too. No –" he put out his hand to Rose who was standing up to try and help him – "you are my guests. Sit and rest. This I can do. Excuse me." Abe slowly walked towards his kitchen. Red followed him.

Sam watched him walk out of the room. There was something about Abe's voice that she liked. Maybe it was his accent; it made his English sound different – special, and more interesting. Sam tapped her forehead as, mentally, she ran through the few things she knew

about Abe. The words on the back of the old photo were in Polish, so he must have grown up speaking Polish and learned English later. This impressed Sam. She'd always thought that being able to speak more than one language was way cool. Sam badly wanted to be able to speak Spanish as beautifully as Olga. *Hmm,* she thought, *maybe I could ask Abe to teach me Polish. That might be a fun way for him to get to know me and me to get to know him.* Sam's inner dialogue was cut short by Danni letting loose one huge honker of a sneeze.

"Bless you, Honey," said Rose as she pulled a tissue from her bag. "Where did *that* come from?"

"I don't know." Danni rubbed her neck. "My throat is getting all scratchy."

Rose frowned as she studied her elder daughter's face. "You do look kind of blotchy, but hang in there, Sweetie. You're still exhausted from the long trip. Maybe your blood sugar is low; have a cookie with your tea and I'm sure you'll feel better."

Danni sneezed again as she nodded. Sam was about to make a joke to try and get Danni to laugh when Abe popped his head back into the room.

"Would anyone like milk with their tea?"

"Yes, please!" Sam answered as she leaped up. "Let me help."

Abe smiled at his new assistant. Sam thought that he seemed to enjoy giving her instructions about what to put on the tray and how to stack the teacups. Once everything was prepared, Abe reached for the tray.

"Wait a second," she said. "I'll carry that, but I want to show you something first." She reached inside the neckline of her T-shirt and pulled out the chain with the simple ring from the shoebox. "Does this look familiar?"

Abe leaned in and squinted to look at the little ring. He drew in a sharp breath.

"Yes," he replied softly, "I know this ring. I gave it to my Golda; it was both her engagement and wedding ring. I promised her someday I would get one much better, but she told me that she didn't need anything fancy."

Sam felt guilty for making Abe sad, but she was excited that she'd guessed correctly. "Um, Mom has the photo we found that was with this ring. Let's go look at it!" She lifted the heavy tray and cautiously walked out of the kitchen.

Back in the living room, Danni was still sneezing. Sam carefully set down the tray; she tried to pour the tea, but it was clear she was about to make a mess. Rose swiftly took the teapot out of her daughter's unsteady hands.

"How about I pour the tea and, Samantha, you pass out the cookies?"

Sam glanced over at her grandfather to see if he was disappointed in her, but he wasn't looking at her – his focus was on Danni.

"Allow me to get you some water," he said as he headed back to the kitchen.

"What's up with you?" Sam hissed at her sister.

"I really don't know," Danni wheezed back. "I feel rotten."

Abe returned with the water and everyone watched Danni struggle to drink it.

"Abe." Rose put down the teapot and reached out her hand to him. "Please accept my sincere apology for cutting this visit short, but Danni appears to be having a spell of some kind. I feel it's best we get her back to the hotel as quickly as possible."

"But we just got here!" Sam blurted out. "We didn't

even get to drink the tea!"

Abe put his hand on Sam's shoulder. "No, your mother is correct. Your sister is not looking well."

"But, but, but we didn't get to talk about anything!" she sputtered. "We didn't get to talk at all about Dad or you and how you got lost – *nothing*!" Sam whipped around to face her sister. "Come on, Danni," she begged, "tell Mom you want to stay a little longer!"

"Samantha Sue." Rose's voice had an edge to it. "We will figure out a way to see your grandfather again *tomorrow*." She turned to Abe. "If that's all right with you."

"Come any time tomorrow!" Abe moved to the door. "Red and I will be here."

Robert and Olga helped Danni out of the cottage and into the limo. Rose assured Abe that she would get him a message about tomorrow. Sam lagged behind.

Abe, with Red at his heels, stood with Sam. She wanted to ask if he was bothered about their leaving so soon, but couldn't find the words. Just as she was about to join everyone in the limo, Abe put his hand on her shoulder.

"Don't worry," he said kindly. "I promise we will

talk. There is much to discuss. You have questions, I have questions, but there is time. You take care of your sister first."

He patted Sam on the head as he studied her face for a moment, before mumbling, "She had green eyes. I see your mother and sister have blue, but you, you have the green eyes of my Golda."

Sam grinned from ear to ear. She was too thrilled to speak. Her heart was beating a million miles an hour. Her grandfather saw a little bit of her grandmother in her! It boggled Sam's mind how she could be so excited about *this* and so upset with her sister all at the same time.

CHAPTER 12

Click click click, clack clack click.

This has to be a wicked-quick post; I'm not supposed to be writing right now. We got back to our hotel about five minutes ago, after having a WAY TOO SHORT meeting with Grandpa Abe. Can you believe it? My whole life (all twelve years and eleven months of it) I didn't know I *had* a grandpa, then I find him, we fly to the other side of the planet to see him, and I only get *a couple of stinky minutes* to talk to him?!?! HOW UNFAIR IS THAT???

WHY did we leave so quickly? Here's why. Danni *claimed* she was sick. She started sneezing as soon as we got into our grandfather's house. I think she was faking. She began to feel better as soon as we got back into the limo — well, maybe not the exact minute we got back in, but not long after. Doesn't that seem suspicious?

Nobody said much of anything on the ride back here to the hotel; Mom has ordered us all to be in Danni's room in the next sixty seconds for a family meeting. I cannot be late! OOPS! I just checked the clock and I've been typing for forty-eight seconds. I'm leaving NOW!

Sam and Olga raced into Danni's hotel room, where they found her sitting on the sofa, laughing at whatever was on the TV. There was no more sneezing or wheezing. Feeling very suspicious, Sam slumped into a chair opposite her sister.

Rose switched off the TV, gracefully span around, and clasped her hands in front of her. It seemed to Sam that her mom had something special to say but couldn't

find the right words, so Sam piped up with what was on her mind.

"Mom, don't you find it *interesting* how Danni was fine all morning until we got to Abe's house, gets sick after we'd been inside for only a few minutes, and then is totally fine again by the time we get back to the hotel?" she asked pointedly.

Danni gawked at her little sister. "Excuse me? What's your problem?"

Sam tried to act all innocent. "No problem. I'm just saying that it's hard not to notice how quickly you bounced back from being *so sick* that we had to leave before even having a cup of tea with our grandpa, and now you're sitting here totally *peachy keen*."

"Wait a minute." Rose's voice had that strong edge that let everyone know they needed to listen. "I believe I can clear up this entire *misunderstanding*."

"In my professional opinion," Robert chimed in, "our Danni here was overcome by the emotional impact of the moment. It caused her artistic sensibilities to overload, thus triggering an asthma attack."

Rose, Danni, Sam and even Olga completely ignored him.

"When Danni was a toddler," Rose said, "not more than two years old, your father…" She nodded at her daughters…"brought home a puppy. He always loved animals." Rose let out a small sigh before turning to Danni. "And you thought that cute little mutt was the greatest thing in the whole world. But after a couple of minutes, you began to sneeze. We bathed the puppy, but even after we'd scrubbed him so clean we could have eaten off his back, you still couldn't be around him without having breathing problems. We had to accept that you were allergic to dogs and find that puppy another home." Rose made sure she caught Sam's eye.

Frowning, Sam came back with, "But that was *years* ago! Danni's totally grown up! There's no way she could still be allergic to dogs!"

"Samantha," Rose said firmly, "I believed she had outgrown her allergy by now – that often happens – but it appears she hasn't. If I'd thought there was any chance Danni would have that reaction, do you think I'd have let her enter Abe's home?"

Sam hopped to her feet. "But this doesn't make sense. I'm not allergic to dogs! I'm not allergic to *anything*! I'm at the stables every day with animals and

I've never so much as had a stuffed-up nose! This has to be a mistake!"

Rose shook her head. "There is no mistake, Little Bit. Danni is allergic to dogs – not horses, dogs. It's never been much of a problem up until now, which is why I didn't think about it straight away."

"Mom!" Sam wailed. "Now it's a *huge* problem! If Danni really is allergic to dogs, then how can Abe and Red come live with us?"

As soon as the words escaped her lips, Sam wanted to kick herself. She hadn't meant to spill her guts like that. In fact, she hadn't even realized that this idea had been brewing in the back of her mind. Yet, once she heard the idea, it didn't sound so crazy. Why shouldn't her grandpa live with them? It wasn't as if they didn't have the room. That ridiculous mansion they were stuck in for at least another two years while they completed the contract for the reality show had *more* than enough bedrooms.

Danni rolled her eyes. "You have got to be kidding! You are *not* thinking of bringing someone into our home, grandpa or no grandpa, who you've known for a whole five minutes!" She folded her arms. "Mother,

you *are* going to tell her she's being flakier than a Flake bar, aren't you?"

"Mom!" Sam whined. "You aren't going to let her talk about me like that, are you?"

"I'm almost eighteeen," Danni snapped. "I can say whatever I want as long as it's *true*!"

Sam shot back with an angry, "Is *not*!"

Rose broke the nasty flow of the moment by loudly clearing her throat. Then, she closed her eyes, put the back of her hand to her forehead, and murmured to herself, "I am calm and in control. I am calm and in control."

Normally, when Rose did something like this, Sam knew it was a signal to chill out immediately or risk getting grounded or banned from her *screens* (computer, TV, iPod), but she was so wound up that there didn't seem to be any way for her to get a grip on her emotions.

Sam stomped about the suite. "I can't believe I finally, *finally* get to have some kind of living, breathing connection to my dad, only to lose it again because of Danni and her made-up allergies! This is bogus! This is baloney! This is—"

"This is *me* sending *you* to your room, young lady!" Rose interjected.

Sam wanted to argue, but thought better of it once she saw the expression on her mom's face. Storming over to the door, Sam let out a grunt as she accidentally kicked the foot of a solid wooden armchair. Biting the insides of her cheeks to stop herself sobbing, Sam bolted out of Danni's suite and into the hallway. Then, instead of turning and going to her room, she went to the lift and pushed the "down" button.

She cringed as she heard the door of Danni's suite open. Desperately trying to play it cool, she turned her head slowly to see who had come out and was stunned to find Michi and Lou videotaping her as she stood there, staring at them.

Trying to pretend they weren't there, Sam tapped her toe impatiently. Why was the lift taking so long to arrive? Sam knew if Rose caught her disobeying a direct order, she probably would be grounded, lose all her screens, and be on the first flight home, but she just didn't care. She was going to hop in a cab and go back out to see Abe again right now.

The lift doors opened. Sam rushed in, pushed the

button for the hotel lobby, and continued to try to ignore Michi and Lou as they got in too and went on filming her. When they reached the ground floor, Sam pushed her way out and ran to the big, heavy doors.

As she prepared to lean against the doors, someone outside pulled them open. Sam stumbled out into the daylight, landing on her knees. The doorman helped her stand and tried to brush the dust off her, but when she saw Lou and Michi running towards her, Sam took off down the street as fast as she could. She was just about to turn the corner when she heard Michi hollering. Looking back, she saw poor, chubby Lou, doubled-over, desperately trying to breathe.

"Sam," Michi called out, "don't do this to Lou. He won't give up and it'll kill him. Come back. Blu wants to talk to you."

Even though she wanted to keep going, Sam was worried about Lou. She hurried back to where Michi was using her free hand to wave cool air on her wheezing partner, while her other hand was still holding the camera and videotaping Sam.

Seeing Lou struggle made Sam feel super-guilty. She joined Michi in using her hands to fan the big guy as he fought to get air into his lungs. At last he returned to a normal human colour and stood up straight again. Giving Sam a reassuring pat on the shoulder, Lou whispered, "Thank you," before lifting up his boom and returning to his job.

Sam felt pretty dumb. There she was, standing on the sidewalk down the block from her hotel, without a sweater, not having any idea where to go or what to do. She felt rotten for almost giving Lou a heart attack, she'd been pretty heartless to her own sister, *and* she was still being videotaped. She peered directly into the camera.

"Okay, Blu," she said, "you wanted to chat?"

Michi handed over her earpiece. As Sam wrapped it round her ear, she heard Blu's worried voice asking, "I hope you can understand that I'm speaking to you as your friend when I ask, *what's the matter with you?* You are so much smarter than this! If your mother finds out that you tried to run away instead of going to your room – whoa, man! – I'm afraid to imagine how mad she'll be. Get yourself back into that hotel and up to your room *pronto*!"

"But, Blu," Sam whined, "you don't understand!"

"But, Sam," he whined right back, "I get it. You met your grandfather and you don't want to lose this connection to your father! Am I close?"

Pouting, Sam nodded.

"And you created this daydream where your grandfather turned out to be a perfect grandpappy who'd move into your house, and make you breakfast, and sing you lullabies, and you all would live happily ever after, yeah?"

Embarrassed, Sam whispered, "Maybe."

Blu's tone lightened. "That's a great *fantasy*, but you need to deal with *reality*. Your gramps is an old man. You don't know him and he doesn't know you. Just being blood related isn't enough to make a *family*; you need to learn who you both are as *people* – the kinds of things you like, what you think about the world. You need to help each other catch up on a lifetime's worth of the stuff that makes each of us unique."

Sam rubbed her nose to stop herself from crying. Blu was absolutely, totally, one-hundred per cently right; but what he said sounded really difficult. She handed Michi the earpiece and sadly shuffled back towards the hotel.

Everyone in the lobby noticed the sad girl being followed by the camera crew, but Sam was too obsessed with her own thoughts to care. She didn't even see Mr. Walker striding towards her from the other side of the lobby. He caught up with her as she pressed the lift call button.

"Good day, Miss Devine."

Sam didn't make eye contact as she sullenly replied, "Hi."

Mr. Walker held out a small box. "This arrived at the front desk for you."

"For me? Uh, thank you." Sam took the box and stepped into the lift. As it slowly went up to the top floor, she opened the card attached to the lid. It read:

Great photos! Thanks a million for sharing!
Your #1 Fan

Completely confused, Sam opened the box and was stunned to find *her* digital camera! Oh! She realized she hadn't seen it since she and Olga had been taking pictures in front of Buckingham Palace. Some nice person must have found it, looked at the photos, recognized her and her family, and dropped it off at the hotel, which – thanks to the paparazzi – everyone in London seemed to know was where Danni Devine was staying. As she got out of the lift, she mindlessly scrolled through all the images on the little camera. There were a lot of photos – a lot of *great* photos – in that digital camera.

Hey! Sam's thoughts started spinning. *What did Blu say? Help Grandpa Abe catch up on a lifetime's worth of the stuff?* She let herself into her suite, raced over to the desk, and got right to work. As she plugged the camera into her computer, she picked up the phone and called her mom to ask if, instead of them going back out to Abe's house, he could come to the hotel tomorrow morning.

CHAPTER 13

Even though she'd stayed up working on her special Grandpa Abe surprise all night, Sam bounced around the hotel conference room like a rubber ball. She kept walking around in a circle, from her computer to the external speakers, to the projector, then over to the giant screen on the wall.

Danni yawned as she stumbled into the room, plopped into a chair, and took a swig of water before holding up her hand and announcing to her sister, "Before you ask me *for the fiftieth time*: it's only five minutes since you last demanded to know what time it was, I do not know why Robert is so late bringing

Abe here to the hotel, but I'm sure everything is fine, and, *yes*, I went back up to my room and took an allergy pill."

Continuing to circle the room, Sam clapped her approval. Danni gave another loud yawn. She stretched out her arms to try to get her blood flowing, and was startled when Sam, still racing about, walked into her left arm.

"Little Bit," she grumbled, "you've *got* to chill. This little multimedia show you put together is hot! It's killer! It totally *rules*! Now, sit and mellow like Jell-O. You're making me dizzy. I didn't make the best first impression with Abe yesterday, and I'd hate for our second visit to begin with me hurling all over him."

Perhaps it was her nervous energy, or the lack of sleep, but whatever the reason, Sam found Danni's comment surprisingly funny and she giggled her head off. The next minute Rose swept in, followed by three hotel workers bringing in trays of coffee, tea and a variety of muffins, and sat next to Danni.

"Samantha Sue," Rose said as she looked around the room, "I have no idea what all these machines actually do, but it certainly appears impressive."

"You'll be blown away when you see the show she put together, Mrs. Devine," asserted Olga as she walked in carrying a tray with a large silver bowl and a covered plate. "Sam is a rock star when it comes to computers."

"Oh. So, my sister's a *rock* star, is she?" Danni asked light-heartedly. "That sounds way cooler than just being a plain old *pop* star." She elbowed her sister. "Can I be in your fan club?"

Embarrassed, Sam joked, "No fan club. Keep your love, just throw me your money!"

From the entryway, a voice called out, "Throwing money is easy; it's the catching that takes skill."

At first, Sam got even *more* embarrassed, but the glint in Abe's eye let her know that he was playing along with her. She greeted him and gave Red a pat on the head as Robert gently guided the two visitors over to a big, comfortable chair with a fluffy blanket on the floor next to it.

Once Abe and Red had settled into their spots, Olga regally carried the silver tray over and set it next to the dog. She lifted the lid to reveal a large steak bone. Abe thanked her for being so thoughtful.

 173

Olga grinned but refused to take the credit. "It was Sam's idea," she explained.

"In fact," Rose spoke as she handed Abe a cup of tea, "the presentation you are about to see is completely Samantha's creation. She put together this little show to help you learn more about us, the crazy people who've just popped into your life." She turned to Sam. "Okay, Little Bit. The floor is yours."

After having spent the whole night putting together the perfect multimedia presentation for her grandpa, Sam realized she hadn't thought of how to introduce it to him. For a second, she considered thanking her friend Blu for helping her find all the pictures and video clips of the family from the internet – turns out being famous makes it easy to find all kinds of stuff *on* and *about* you – and then pull it all into her multimedia spectacular. If Michi hadn't come to Sam around midnight and given her one of her extra earpieces so Blu could coach Sam throughout the creative process, she'd never have managed to put it all together.

Sam glanced up to see everyone in the room staring at her. Without saying a word, she forced a grin, threw her arm out towards the giant screen on the wall, and backed away until she reached the computer.

The next twenty-five minutes flew by. Photos of Sam and Danni as babies, kids, and then as they were today flashed by along with clips from *The Devine Life* TV show and snippets of Danni performing. Next came a video of Danni speaking directly into the camera, explaining about her dog allergy, and another video section where Rose described her husband, how she'd loved him, and how he had died too young. She held up the small photo of her and her husband kissing at their wedding. The last two minutes featured Sam talking about how she wanted Abe to know the Devine family better so he could decide for himself how much he did (or did not) want to have them in his life. On screen, Sam admitted, "Being famous is really weird. Trying to be normal when people are chasing you because a photo of your family can sell for lots of money is majorly bizarre. If you feel that our lives are too wacky and you'd rather have your space and not get *too* involved with us, we'll be sad…*I'll* be sad, but I'll understand. A good friend helped me get a grip on the fact that I can't *demand* you be the grandpa I imagined

in my head, any more than I can be the perfect granddaughter you pictured in your head…if you ever imagined a…I mean…if you'd thought." Sam sighed and mumbled, "Um – *the end*." Then, she waved and the video faded to black.

Robert turned the lights back on. No one was sure what to say. The stillness was broken by a howling yawn from Red; everyone laughed and relaxed.

Abe gave his dog a rub on the head. "Don't worry, Samantha," he said, "Mr. Red is not much of a movie critic. It was a wonderful show; thank you for working so hard to let me see into your hearts. I am lucky to have you as my family."

Sam beamed. She was so pleased that she couldn't speak for fear that she'd bawl.

"Abe," Rose said delicately, "we are all truly sorry that yesterday didn't go too well. Sam worked very hard to make this show for you because it's through her writing and computer skills that she best communicates her most personal thoughts. It would mean the world to the girls if you could share some of your personal thoughts and some family history. You see, I have my memories of Daniel, but Danni was only

five when he passed away, and Sam never got to meet him. You are their closest connection to him. Anything you could share about yourself and Golda would be much appreciated."

"Yes, yes." He nodded. "I understand. I will do my best to remember. This is not easy; I have not spoken of such matters for many years."

His eyes clouded over as he spoke about how he and Golda had been born in the same little town in Poland. Their mothers knew each other, but they themselves had not been friends. They did not become close until some years after the war had ended. By then, Abe was twenty and Golda was almost eighteen.

"We were living in a special place where they put Jews who were young and lost – Golda and I were both of these things. We waited there for our families to find us; as we waited we shared memories of our village back in Poland, the great town park, the tall trees, and the man with the cart who would sell ice creams to us children. Talking of such things felt nice and almost normal again."

"*Föhrenwald!*" Sam jumped in. "The displaced persons camp! That's where you were living, right?"

Abe nodded. "Yes, Föhrenwald. It was not fancy, but it was a safe place for those who had spent so much of the war being scared and alone; Golda and I had both been hidden with other families when we were very young. I was almost six years with a family in Austria. I had no idea where to find my parents, so I stayed and waited at Föhrenwald. The people there made sure we got food and clean clothes; they tried to help us to decide where to go next. We had no reason to stay in Germany, where the camp was, but we heard stories that made us think it would not be wise to go back to Poland."

This confused Sam. She wanted to ask how Abe had ended up in Germany in the first place, but decided against interrupting him again.

"Golda and I married at the Föhrenwald," Abe continued. "We stayed there as long as we could, but then it was decided to close the camp and we had to find another place to live. This was late in the 1950s. America was a dream we heard on the radio or saw in the movies. We applied for visas, and as we waited for these papers, we learned that Golda was going to have a baby. This made us very happy, but it also meant we needed to get to America sooner so the baby could be born there, as an American."

Abe started to cough. Both Sam and Robert got him water. Abe reached out and Sam shoved *her* glass of water into his hand.

"Thank you." Abe got his breathing back under control and continued.

"When we got our papers to live in America, we were very happy. We had very little money, but I managed tickets for the first ship to America that would accept our travel visas, the *Queen Frederica*. The ship was to leave from Naples, in Italy, for New York in thirty days. I decided that while we waited, I should go back to Poland and try to find anyone from our families; Golda wanted to come, but because she was pregnant, I worried that this quick trip would be too much for her. I promised I would be back in time, and that, if for some reason I was late for the train to Italy, I would meet Golda at the dock. I promised I would be there with her on the ship."

Abe tapped his fingers on the table. Sam couldn't tell if he had forgotten what happened next or was remembering too well and it was upsetting him.

Focusing on his glass of water, Abe returned to his story. "I took the train to Poland, and then had to walk to our little town. It took two days, which was not bad, but I got into a problem. As I walked, I met with a group of friendly people. They had built a good fire and let me join them." Abe used his hands to act out what he was describing. "I sat close to the fire to warm my hands and feet, but a…" He seemed confused. "I can't remember the word in English. A hot thing that flies out of a fire, what do you call that?"

"An ash?" offered Rose.

"An ember?" said Robert.

"A cinder?" suggested Sam.

"Cinder!" Abe snapped his fingers. "That's the thing. So I am sitting and warming at the fire, when a cinder flies up and lands in my eye. It burned, but I didn't think much about it until the next morning when I woke up in horrible pain. My whole head felt about to explode. I couldn't walk because I was shaking with fever; my eye was infected and I was in bad shape. The friendly people took me to the nearest hospital. There, they gave me medicines and saved me and my eye."

Abe paused. He rubbed his nose. Sam gasped; she recognized that *she* did that very same thing whenever she was trying to find exactly the right words to say.

Another quick sip of water and Abe returned to his story. "Once my fever was gone and I was strong enough to talk, I discovered I was very, very late. As soon as I could walk again, I hurried back to the Föhrenwald camp, but no Golda. She'd left me a note saying she would be waiting for me at the ship, so I got on the first train down to Italy to join her. I was too late; I missed the sailing of our ship. It made me feel terrible, but still, I thought that Golda would have left another letter for me somewhere. I searched and asked; it was hard because I spoke only Polish, German, and the little English I had learned in the Föhrenwald – no Italian. Finally I found a man who worked in the port who understood me. He told me that Golda had been there, but a telegram had come in saying that there had been a death on the ship; a woman travelling alone had had her baby too early and both the woman and the baby had died at sea."

"I'm so sorry, Abe," Rose said gently. "That must have been heartbreaking."

He shook his head. "It was unbelievable. I did not believe the man – I got mad and kept asking, searching, but what was there to find? There was no Golda, no baby, no letter. What could I do? I was without a home or a family or travel papers. Anyway, I did not want to go to America without my Golda, so I wandered. Eventually, I made my way here, to England. I met a nice man, a veterinarian. I had a way with animals, so he gave me a job. He trained me to be his assistant; over the years, I learned and became a veterinarian myself and took over his business. This became my life, helping animals. I never had any idea that I had a child in the world. I am sad I never got to know him, but when I see you lovely ladies, I can tell that my son became a good man who married a fine woman and had beautiful children."

There was so much that Sam wanted to ask about, but her attention had been totally drawn to his mention of animals and how he had a way with them. *She'd always been awesome with animals!*

"Heavens, Abe!" exclaimed Rose. "It's remarkable to hear your end of the story. All we knew was that Daniel, your son, had been born on the ship, but his birth mother, Golda, died in labour. Mrs. Anna Devine was a passenger returning to America; apparently she was there when Daniel was born and begged the captain to let her take the boy. As the baby appeared to have no other family, the captain agreed to her request, rather than hand the baby over to an orphanage. For whatever comfort it brings you, Abe, please know that Daniel had a wonderful childhood."

"My memories of my dad are all amazing," chimed in Danni. "I remember him smiling a lot and singing to me all the time."

"I can assure you, Abe," Rose tittered, "*none* of Danni's singing abilities come from me or my side of the family."

Abe smiled in understanding. "That gift did not come from me either; it was my Golda whose singing was magic. Yes, she was my songbird."

"I like birds!" Sam practically exploded. "I like all kinds of birds and cats and dogs, but especially *horses*! I think horses are the greatest animals in the whole world! I've *always* loved horses! Do *you*? Love horses? You said you'd always had a way with animals. Does that include horses? Did you have a lot of animals growing up?"

Abe looked over at Sam, but something was different.

His expression was strained, and he struggled to stand, while mumbling about needing to get back home.

Robert and Sam rushed over to help and everyone followed as Abe slowly worked his way out of the conference room, through the hotel doors, and out to the waiting limousine.

Rose, Danni and Olga all wished Abe and Red a genuinely fond goodbye, and stepped back. Sam, however, threw herself into the limo.

"Please, Abe," she pleaded, "I'm sorry I bothered you. I have so many things I want to ask you. I know I can be too much sometimes. Please don't be mad!"

"Do not be bothered with an old man's moods," he said tenderly. "When too many memories come too quickly, it can make me sleepy. All is good."

Abe patted Sam on the head. It reminded her of the way he showed affection to Red. It gave her the confidence to push for the thing she really wanted.

Click click click, clack clack click.

Somehow I totally freaked out Grandpa Abe this morning, BUT I did get him to agree to let me come out to see him tomorrow morning before we sail home. That's right – we leave England *tomorrow*! I cannot believe it's already time for us to go home. We just got here! I was majorly worried I'd never see Abe again, but Mom *promised* me that she'd pay for him to come and visit soon. That made me feel a little better, but still...

Leaving tomorrow also means that it's almost time for Danni's big showdown with horrible Harley. It was THE topic at dinner tonight. Poor Danni is wickedly worked-up. I'm ashamed – I've been so caught up in the Grandpa Abe drama that I'd totally forgotten about the concert; I hope that doesn't make me a terrible little sister. I'll make it up to Danni somehow!

Since dinner, Olga and I have been in our room playing video games and talking about all the cool stuff over here. I'm bummed we never did get to see the whole "Changing of the Guard" thing, but hey – it gives me something specific to look forward to on our *next* trip! (grin)

Whoops! Mom just yelled through the door that she's about to come in and check that Olga and I are all packed and ready for bed. I haven't put a single thing back in my suitcase yet! I SO gotta go!!

More soon!!

CHAPTER 14

Sam fidgeted in the back of the limo as her mind bounced all over the place – from worrying about Danni to trying to figure out how best to use her last hour with her grandpa. It had been a mess of a morning.

Everything had started out so great. Rose had burst into Sam and Olga's room with a tray of fresh muffins and hot cocoa. But seconds later, a blotchy, itchy Danni had run in screeching and scratching. Her face was puffed up like popcorn; her eyes were beetroot red. It appeared she was having a world-class allergy attack.

Sam freaked out when she remembered that she

hadn't changed clothes after giving Red hugs yesterday morning, and then she'd hugged her sister at bedtime last night. Her mom, however, refused to let Sam blame herself.

"This has nothing to do with allergies," Rose had explained. "It's Danni's nerves working overtime." She shook her head and muttered, "Between the schmooze cruise and Harley, it's a miracle we aren't all covered in blotches and blemishes."

For a moment, Rose had seriously considered cancelling the visit to Abe, but Robert had stepped in and saved the day. He assured Rose that everything was on schedule; he'd get another car to take Sam and Olga to Virginia Water, and then to the dock well before the ship's departure time.

Sam was going to thank him, but before she could, he had snarled a snarky warning to her about not messing up his perfect schedule, so she'd clammed up.

"Hey." Olga brought Sam back to the present. "You look *way* serious. Don't worry; your grandfather won't be upset about just you and me coming out. He's going to be totally happy to get to spend a little extra time with you, and besides— "

Olga was interrupted by the ringing of her cellphone.

"Mom!" Olga yelled into the tiny handset. "Hang on. Hey, Sam, it's my mom!"

The call gave Sam an opportunity to scoot up to the front of the limo, where Michi and Lou were busy doing their jobs.

Sam reached out her hand and asked Michi if she could borrow her earpiece to talk to Blu. Michi handed it over and Sam quickly popped it into her ear.

"Blu," she whispered into Lou's microphone, "can you hear me?"

"Are you nuts?" Blu's voice came directly into her head. "You want to chat *now*?"

"Aw, don't be mad at me," Sam whimpered. "How can I best say goodbye to Grandpa Abe without getting too mushy, but still let him know that I really and truly do want to keep in touch?"

"Tell him *exactly that*," Blu answered.

"Oh. Oh!" She thumped herself on the head for not seeing the obvious. "Duh!"

"Okay, Dweeblet." Blu laughed. "Now, sit yourself back and quit talking to me; you aren't supposed to acknowledge I'm around, remember?"

 189

Sam saluted into the camera. "Sir! Yes, sir! Over and out, sir!"

She started to hand the earpiece back to Michi, but then quickly pulled it back for one last question.

"Why are you guys following me and Olga today? Wouldn't it be more interesting if you stuck with Danni?"

Blu sighed before answering. "Yes, it would. But with your sister being covered in nervous hives, your mom requested we give Danni a break for a couple of hours."

Sam nodded. "Yeah, I guess that makes sense."

Blu's laughter filled her whole head. "I'm glad you approve. Now give the earpiece back to Michi and go back to living your life."

"Mom!" Olga shouted into the phone. "We're pulling up outside Sam's granddad's house. I have to go now! I love you too. I miss you too. Bye!"

Not waiting for the driver to get out and open the door for them, the girls hopped out as soon as the limo stopped. They reached the front door and as Sam reached out to knock, it flew open and there stood Abe, waiting for them with a big smile.

Sam immediately babbled about poor Danni and

how badly she and Rose felt about not being able to come out to say goodbye. Abe took the news well – his smile only dimmed a little – then he demanded everyone (including Michi and Lou) find a comfortable place to sit in the living room.

As Sam sat, she pulled a napkin out of her pocket. "Abe," she asked, "may I give Red a piece of muffin from my breakfast? I thought he might like it."

The old man chuckled. "It appears you have a good friend in our young Samantha, Mr. Red." He smiled at Sam. "Yes, you may give him the muffin. Normally I am strict with his diet, but a special treat every now and then is nice."

Sam slipped onto the floor. She scratched Red's back as he happily ate the muffin. Abe watched her before asking, "You have a gift for getting along with animals, yes?"

"Oh, *so* yes!" Sam exploded. "I *love* animals, *all* of them!"

Abe was pleased. "Loving animals is a sign of a good heart."

Sam was excited that she and her grandfather seemed to be connecting. "One of my dreams is to ride

a horse in the Olympics," she gushed. "I know a lot about horses. I'm sure there's a ton more I could learn with a grandpa who's a veterinarian – I mean, I'd like to learn more, and you, being my grandpa, could maybe teach me, and…"

Real smooth, Sam, she said to herself as she realized she was babbling, *you finally have your grandpa's undivided attention and you're acting like a total bonehead. Think of something smart to say!*

She stood up. "How about we have that cup of tea we never got to finish the other day? I'd love to help you make it!"

Amused by Sam's enthusiasm, Abe slapped his knee. "That sounds nice; to the kitchen we go. Our friend, Olga," he said with a smile, "you will join us, yes?"

Abe got right to work filling his small kettle with water. Olga spied a box of dog biscuits and pointed it out to Sam. She slipped her hand inside, pulled one out, and quickly tossed it over to Red. The dog leaped and caught it in mid-air. Abe saw all this through the corner of his eye.

"He may be old like me," he said, "but my Red can still jump when he wants to."

Feeling relaxed and happy, Sam asked, "Why did you name him Red when he is every colour a dog could be *except* red?"

Abe's eyes clouded over. His friendly, open mood seemed to vanish. Sam was way sorry she'd asked the question, but still, why would such an honest, innocent query be so bothersome to her grandpa? Trying to make everything all right again, Sam reached down to pet Red. The old dog happily lay flat on his back. In the midst of this delicious tummy scratching, he farted loudly, seriously smelling up the kitchen.

Both girls tried to ignore the dog's gas, but they couldn't keep their giggles from bursting out. At first, Abe was focused on opening windows and waving a towel to make the horrible smell go away, but once he heard their laughter, he joined right in.

With his strange mood over, Abe returned to the tea. As he put the kettle on to boil, he began to hum. Sam enjoyed the tune, but she didn't know it. Olga, however, recognized the song immediately.

"'Pennies From Heaven'!" she cried out with delight. "I love that song! My grandmother plays it on her piano every time I visit."

Abe seemed surprised by Olga's outburst; it was as if he hadn't even realized that he'd been humming. "Yes, this 'Pennies From Heaven' was Golda's favourite song. It was funny to me how a person who never learned English could be so in love with an English song and sing it over and over. A friend in the camp wrote out the words translated into Polish; Golda loved this idea of pennies dropping down from the clouds." He shook his head. "How she would smile as she sang this song, no matter how bad things were."

Abe finished making the tea while Sam looked around for the cups and saucers. She opened several cupboards before finding the right one; however, there appeared to be two different sets of china.

"Which cups should we use, Mr. Zab— Abe, I...I..." Sam tripped over her tongue. She grimaced. "I know you don't want me to call you 'Mr. Zabinski', but I just can't call you by your first name. It sounds way too much like we're friends. I'm not saying we aren't friends, but I like thinking that we're more than friends, because we are, aren't we?"

Abe gently replied, "Yes. We are more than friends. I think it would be nice if you were to call me

'Grandfather Abe' or 'Grandpa Abe'. How does that sound?"

Beaming with happiness, Sam answered, "It sounds wicked!"

Abe scratched his head as he asked Olga, "*Wicked? Is good?*"

Olga nodded seriously. "Oh, yes. Wicked is *very* good."

Clasping his hands together, Abe grinned. "Good. Then pull up a stool and join your Grandpa Abe in a cup of this wicked tea."

Sam had never been a big fan of tea before, but after tasting Grandpa Abe's brew, she was hooked for life. It made her very happy to see Olga enjoying her tea as well. The time passed quickly as the three shared likes, dislikes, and silly jokes. Sam was about to ask for a third cup of tea, but was cut off by a knocking at the front door.

"Excuse me, young ladies," Abe said as he shuffled out of the room. "I'll get it."

A minute later, he returned to the kitchen with the limo driver.

"My dears," Abe said, "this gentleman here explained

to me that you need to be leaving to go to your boat now."

"Not yet!" Sam begged. "We haven't finished our tea! Five more minutes!"

"Samantha," Abe gently admonished his granddaughter, "I don't want to be the cause of you getting into any trouble with your mother. The boat will not wait for anyone, not even you."

Sam bit her bottom lip to stop it from quivering. She knew the correct thing to do was get into the limo so she'd be on time to meet her mom and Danni at the ship, but she had this overwhelming fear that this would be the last time she'd ever meet with Grandpa Abe, and there were still way too many unanswered questions.

As Abe walked the girls to the front door, Sam grabbed Olga by the elbow.

"Listen," she whispered, "I need you to back me up on something. You with me?"

Concern surfaced in Olga's eyes, but she gave her best friend a quick nod and a confused, but loyal, smile.

As everyone walked outside, Sam loudly proclaimed that she needed to use the bathroom. She hurried back inside the cottage, locked herself in the bathroom, pulled out her cellphone, and froze. Who could she call? The idea swirling around in her brain was both brilliant and demented. She couldn't ask for help (or permission) from her mom – she might say no and that would be the end of it. Robert? *No way.* Blu? Sure, if they were back in America, Blu could totally put this together – but he didn't know anybody over here in England. In frustration, Sam shoved her hand in her back pocket and felt something hard and cold. It was the key to her hotel room. She should have given that back to Mr. Walker. Oh! *Mr. Walker!*

Mr. Walker took Sam's phone call. She babbled on about how she knew she was asking a lot, but since he was the manager of *the* most exclusive hotel in London, he'd know the right people to contact for something this major. Mr. Walker asked Sam to hold the line. Within minutes, he returned to tell her that her fantastic scheme was arranged and ready to go. Flustered with excitement, Sam couldn't thank Mr. Walker enough. Then, with her heart beating so hard it actually hurt, she ran back outside to where Olga, Grandpa Abe, Red, Michi, Lou and the limo driver were all waiting.

"Grandpa Abe," Sam asked casually, "would you like to travel with us on the ship to America?"

At the exact-same moment, Abe, Olga, Lou and even Michi all roared, "*What?!!*"

Sam continued, "See, we're going to be on the ship for four days, and Mom and Danni will be busy prepping for the concert, but Olga and I, we'll be bored to tears. We can totally hang out, and the ship has kennels for dogs and as long as Red has had all his shots, then he can come too and he can have the biggest kennel of them all, and you can both fly home any time you want!"

The offer completely caught Abe off guard. He blinked a dozen times before speaking. "And your mother is acceptable with this?" he asked disbelievingly.

Holding her hand behind her back so he couldn't see her crossed fingers, Sam nodded. "This was all Mom's idea! She promised me that she'd pay for your visit."

Overwhelmed at the unexpected offer of a lifetime, Abe threw his arms in the air.

"I suppose my busy social plans will have to wait!" he exclaimed. "Yes, Samantha, I would be honoured to

join you! I will get my suitcase and the travel papers for Red."

Abe and his dog made it back into the cottage quicker than Sam thought either one of them ever could. She gave herself a pat on the back. That happy feeling, however, quickly melted away as she noticed the many pairs of eyes focused on her.

"I know, I know," she said as she faced Olga, Michi and Lou. "You think I've lost my mind and my mom is going to kill me. It's going to be fine! Come on – would *I* do something like this if I wasn't *completely* confident it was all going to be totally fine?"

Leaping into the limo, Sam sat up straight for a brief second before dropping her head into her hands. *Okay, Samantha Sue*, she said to herself, *don't fall apart now. It will be great! It will...Mom will understand...and forgive me...someday.*

CHAPTER 15

The limo pulled into the dock's VIP gate. Looking ahead, Sam noticed that Rose, Danni and Robert were waiting for her and Olga outside the VIP departure lounge. She saw her mom glaring angrily at Robert. It was plain to see that Robert was doing everything he could to pretend he hadn't noticed. *Uh-oh*, Sam thought, *this does not look like a good time to spring a surprise like Grandpa Abe on Mom.*

She asked the limo driver to pull over a short distance away from the departure lounge to buy herself a minute of thinking time. It didn't do much good; Robert caught sight of the limo as it was pulling over.

Trying to hide his relief, he beelined over. Standing next to the rear passenger door, he waited for someone to exit the vehicle, but no one did. Michi and Lou hopped out from the front and focused their videotaping on the door as well.

"Move it!" Robert tapped on the window. "You're late and your mother is blaming me."

The window rolled down halfway and Sam poked her head out. "How bad a mood is my mom in?" she asked in a hushed voice.

Surprised by the question, Robert just stared down at her.

"This is important!" Sam hissed. "How bad a mood is my mom in *right now*?"

From inside the limo, a voice enquired, "Samantha? Everything is all right, yes?"

When Robert heard Abe's voice, he turned as white as a bed sheet. "You brought your grandfather?" he whispered incredulously. "Because your mother isn't already mad enough at me, is that it? You had to give her a reason to actually want to kill me, right? Because that's what you've done here. Your mother is going to blame me for this."

The car door opened and Sam stepped out. She saw Rose and Danni walking towards the limo. Deciding it was better to get in trouble outside of Abe's range of hearing, she softly pleaded, "Robert, be as mad at me as you want but *please* don't make a scene in front of Grandpa Abe! *Please!* I'll owe you for ever!"

He glared at her, but held his arm out to assist Abe, leaving her free to try and break the news to her mom before Rose got too close and saw Abe without any warning.

Sam threw her arms around Rose. "Hello, Mother! I hope you and Danni had a lovely morning! Olga and I sure did!" Sam was literally jumping all over Rose, trying to keep her attention away from Abe for as long as she could.

Rose was not in the mood for any shenanigans. "Samantha, once you saw that you were running late, why didn't you call and let me know?"

Sam looked her mom straight in the eye. "My fault; my bad. You're right. No excuses. I wasn't thinking."

"Why, Little Bit…" Rose beamed with pride. "That was *very* mature of you! To recognize your mistake and own up to it…is so…so *grown up*! You are becoming

quite th— " Rose froze mid-word when she spied Abe
– and then Red. Without moving, she quietly asked,
"Samantha Sue Devine, why am I seeing your
grandfather and his dog?"

Sam learned long ago that whenever her mother
called her "Samantha Sue Devine", she was in real
trouble. Fearing that Rose was angry enough to refuse
to allow Abe to come on the ship with them, Sam
prepared to throw herself on her mother's mercy and
accept whatever punishment Rose gave her.

"Um…" she stammered, "um, I…I – once you
hear…the story…it's nice…"

"Nice *nothing*," Robert chimed in as he confidently
strode over. "This was sheer genius."

Sam and Rose slowly turned their heads to look
at him.

"It was a *brilliant* publicity move on my part," he
continued. "As we were preparing to leave the hotel this
morning, I learned that Harley was planning a press
conference *just* before we set sail. Recognizing Danni's
need for rest, I was inspired to take care of my client
and still steal Harley's thunder. Mr. Zabinski accepted
my invitation to join us for the cruise across the ocean

in exchange for talking to a couple of reporters and allowing a few photos of him and you all boarding the ship."

Sam had completely stopped breathing. What was going on here? Was Robert covering for her? Was her evil arch-enemy actually helping her out?

"Really, Robert?" Rose asked sarcastically. "It was out of concern for *Danni* that you decided to bring the girls' *grandfather* and his *dog* along for the ride home?"

Robert paused, but a smile remained glued to his face. "Honestly, Rose, if you think about it, how else could this have possibly come together so perfectly?" He let out a terribly fake laugh. "Oh, wait, maybe you think the *kid* here –" he thrust his hand out towards Sam – "took it upon *herself* to invite the old man without your permission?"

Sam's insides were spinning. One minute Robert was playing hero, and the next, he throws her to the lions?

Danni reached out to Rose. "Mom, I'm super-pleased to have Abe along for the trip. I like the idea of getting to perform for my grandfather." She glared at Robert. "Honestly, Robert, I can't believe you'd try

to use a sweet kid like my little sis to take the blame for something you did."

"Danni's right," Rose agreed. "This is a new low, even for you, Mr. Ruebens."

Both Danni and Rose turned their attention towards Abe as he and Olga approached the group. This gave Sam a second to sneak a look up at Robert.

He noticed her eyeballing him. "Don't think I took the heat because I like you," he growled. "There's *no way* I was going to let some snot-nosed kid make me appear foolish in front of a client. Rose may have fired me, but until the concert is over, *I'm* still in control here. *Me* – not you – *me*. Got that?"

Relieved to see the normal, selfish Robert back, Sam smiled at him.

"Knock it off," he hissed. "Go be cute with somebody else."

"*Robert!*" Rose barked. "Hello? I asked you about the cabin you arranged for Abe?"

Without skipping a beat, Robert replied, "Abe will be bunking in my cabin."

"No." Sam shook her head. "He has his own – ouch!"

Robert had stepped on Sam's foot.

"The ship is booked, Rose," he said loudly. "There isn't an empty closet, let alone a cabin, anywhere. My stateroom is huge. I have everything under control."

Sam realized she'd been about to stick her foot in her mouth – if she revealed that Abe actually had his own cabin, booked by Mr. Walker, her mom would realize exactly what had been going on. They would just have to stick to Robert's story.

Again Danni, unknowingly, came to Sam's rescue.

"Mom," she said, "there'll be more than enough room for me and Sam and Olga in my suite. How about the girls stay with me and then Abe can take their cabin?"

Rose gave her older daughter a peck on the cheek. "You are such a doll." Holding out one hand to Abe, she used the other to point towards the massive ship ahead of them. "Abraham Zabinski, would you do me the honour of escorting me and my two daughters across the ocean on that there boat?"

Abe grinned as he walked towards the Premier Class gangplank with Rose Devine on his arm. "The honour is mine," he answered proudly, "but I warn you, getting

these old legs up this steep walkway may take as long as the crossing itself."

Rose twittered her sweet, polite laugh as she assured Abe they had time. Sam watched the two of them strolling up the gangplank with a monster sense of relief. Yet, she also felt a little guilty. She hadn't exactly lied to her mom – still, not confessing that it was *she* who had put all this together didn't seem right. Whatever. She was about to enjoy four awesome days with her *whole* family and her best friend!

Throwing her arms around Danni and Olga, Sam tossed out a challenge. "On the count of three, last one to the top of the gangplank gets last choice of bed in our cabin!"

"Please." Danni acted all bored. "I'm *so* beyond such childish games."

Ignoring her, Sam counted loudly, "One, two, three!"

Danni hip-checked Sam and ran ahead. Sam bolted to get around Olga and catch up with her big sister. Rose and Abe smiled as the girls raced past them.

Danni would have made it up the gangplank to the ship's entryway first if she hadn't turned to see how much

of a lead she had on the other girls. That gave Sam the break she needed to take the lead. She reached the top and lunged head first through the ship's giant doorway.

She whipped around to face Olga and Danni, who weren't far behind.

"Winner!" Sam proclaimed as she danced about the entryway to celebrate her victory.

A nasty voice snarked out. "Winner of what – *Loser of the Year?*"

Sam's jaw dropped as she turned around and saw Harley standing in front of her. And all these people around them in the ship's entryway were reporters and photographers! Harley let out a cold, cruel cackle as cameras clicked and blinding lights flashed everywhere.

"Hey, little Devine!" Harley snapped her fingers. "Quit staring at me or I'm gunna charge your eyeballs rent."

Sam dreamed of marching over and telling Harley that she was mean and rude, but she was afraid. What if Harley's tough rock'n'roll pop star act wasn't an act? Sam had never been in a physical fight; Harley looked like she'd punch somebody just for the fun of it.

"Why so quiet, Shrimp?" Harley taunted Sam.

"I know your *sister's* a major chicken, but I didn't know you were too. Maybe instead of *Little Bit*, we should call you *Little Chick*, or maybe *Chicken Little*, eh?" She turned back to the reporters and mocked Sam, "Oh, the sky is falling! The sky is falling!"

Sam turned red with embarrassment.

Danni stepped forward. "Harley, you leave my sister alone."

"That's cute," Harley sneered, "standing up for the kid. I'm not exactly impressed – still, it's a nice change to see you *standing* at all."

"What are you yapping about?" Danni asked.

"I guess *someone* hasn't seen today's newspaper. Here ya go!" Harley handed a copy to Danni and cackled even louder than before.

Danni glanced down and groaned. Sam peered around her sister to see the huge picture on the front page: it was the photo Sam had snapped on the airplane. In giant letters above it were the words: *Desperately Drinking Danni*. The accompanying story recounted how Danni had been dreadfully drunk and rude throughout the whole flight to London.

"That's a lie!" Sam yelled. "*I* took that picture!

Danni fell because the plane bounced and I...I..." Sam felt sick thinking that she had caused her sister yet *more* public humiliation. "Danni...I'm sorry! I lost my camera, and somebody brought it to our hotel and... and *now* I understand the thank-you note! They must have sold the picture to the newspaper! I can't *believe* anyone would do that! I'm so sorry!"

Danni exhaled a long breath. Sam could tell that it was taking every fibre of strength she had for her not to cry. There had to be *something* Sam could do to get everyone's attention away from her sister. "Harley!" she shouted.

Harley yawned. "Say what you gotta say, Kiddo. I've got a massage in an hour, and *you* –" she leaned in to look down on Sam – "are boring me."

The relief that she'd pulled the focus away from Danni disappeared as Sam panicked with the realization that all eyes were now on her; she couldn't think of a single thing to say or do. Suddenly a loud, threatening growl shattered the silence. Everybody, including Harley flinched. Twisting her head to try and keep one eye on Harley, but still see what had made the noise, Sam saw Red, focusing directly on Harley, at the

top of the gangplank in front of Grandpa Abe, Rose and Robert.

Red growled again, but stopped when Abe patted him on the head. "It's all right, my boy. Be calm. I'm sure the tall girl is only playing with our Samantha. I'm sure there is no threat to our dear girl." Abe smiled at Harley. "This is correct? You are joking, yes?"

Harley studied the elderly man. "Yeah." She patted Sam on the head the same way Abe had done with Red. "Don't worry, Doggie, I'm just messing with the kid."

Harley spun around and left. Rose and Robert swiftly made their way to Sam and Danni, trying to make sure everyone was all right, but Sam was in her own world.

Mr. Red thinks I'm his family, she thought happily. *He was ready to chomp on Harley to protect me!*

Sam could have spent the rest of her day doing nothing more than thinking about how much she was enjoying having a grandpa and a...what was Red to her...a granddoggie? However, Danni brought back the reality of the situation by begging for somebody to get the reporters out of the way so she could go to her cabin and take a nap.

 211

Robert turned on his expensive smile and stepped towards the mass of media people. "Thank you, folks. Today's show is over. I appreciate you're all eagerly awaiting *the* musical event of the year – *Battleship* – the pop showdown between Danni and Harley. Remember, we will be broadcasting live via Today's 2 Cool Teens Network from New York Harbour."

While Robert went on promoting the concert, Rose quietly ordered Danni, Sam, Olga and Abe to follow her as she worked her way out of the room. Everything was going well, until a young reporter yelled out, "Come on, Robert! Enough promoting. What's the scoop with the old bloke? Where'd you find him and the mangey old hound?"

The question hit Sam like a ton of bricks; she whirled back around. "My grandpa is not an 'old bloke' and Red is *not* a 'mangey hound'. Didn't anyone ever teach you that if you can't say anything nice, don't say anything at all?"

Every reporter in the room immediately began pelting Sam with questions, but before she could answer a single one, Rose grabbed her arm and pulled her away.

* * *

Click click click, clack clack click.

SCHMOOZE CRUISE – DAY #1

Call me Sailor Sam (LOL). What I mean is that I'm now typing away at my desk, in my cabin, on this *awesome* ship we're taking back to the US.

Our trip home didn't start off too well. We ended up in the middle of Harley's press conference. It was a mess. Harley was totally snotty – she ripped on Danni and me in front of a ton of reporters. (sigh)

We got out of that disaster and went straight to Mom's cabin for an official family meeting. It was the first time EVER that we had a new family member in a family meeting (Grandpa Abe is travelling with us!! And – even better – Robert is trying to arrange it so that he can stay near us for a couple of weeks before going back to England? Cool, huh? I set a chair and pillow in the hallway so he and Red could be in the meeting

without Danni getting another allergy attack.)

Robert passed out schedules for the rest of the trip and that's when the arguing began.

Mom pitched a fit that Robert had planned so many "meet and greet" sessions for Danni. She thought this crossing from England to New York was going to have *some* family time, but Robert has Danni totally booked doing stuff with her fans. Mom yelled at Robert and stormed out of the cabin. What was funny was that we were in *her* cabin, so two seconds later, she returned and kicked Robert out.

Olga and I ran down to the kennels to make sure that Red had a nice place to sleep. OH MY STARS! His kennel is big and beautiful! Grandpa Abe wanted to have a bed brought down so he could sleep there too, but Olga and I talked him out of that.

I told Grandpa Abe how much I appreciated Red

sticking up for me with Harley. Grandpa Abe totally beamed. I thought it was a perfect time to try to ask again why Red is named Red when he *so* isn't (red, I mean), but I never got the chance! My cellphone rang; it was Mom calling because I was late for Danni's first fan event. Olga and I legged it over there!

When we got there, Danni's fifty fans (all girls) were already lined up. Robert had Olga and me giving each girl a piece of pizza after they'd got a signed photo from Danni. It started out great – but then Harley (grrrr) struts in with her fifty fans and screams how it's *her time* for pizza and autographs so we *must vacate immediately*. Danni tried nicely to get a few more minutes with her fans, but Harley wouldn't listen; she held up her hand right in Danni's face. All of Harley's fans laughed and hooted; Danni left the event in tears.

Olga and I found her in our cabin. She cried that she was over the whole pop star thing. I felt

terrible, but I didn't know what to say. It's a good thing that I have the coolest best friend EVER!

Olga told Danni she understood what she was feeling because she'd spent her life watching her mom and dad deal with fame. Olga sounded super grown-up when she said, "Being famous is a lot like eating chocolate cake – enjoy it a little, and it's fun and yummy, but if it becomes the only thing you care about, pretty soon you'll be so sick of it you'll feel like barfing."

Tomorrow, we have another "schmooze-fest" at breakfast, and then I plan on spending the rest of the day in the kennel with Olga, Grandpa Abe and Red. I still have so many questions! Maybe after a good night's sleep, he'll tell me more about him and Golda – not to mention the whole story behind the naming of Mr. Red.

More soon!!

CHAPTER 16

The next morning, Sam had the toughest time waking up. The rocking of the ship felt so awesome that she thought about staying in bed all day. However, she forgot all about that idea as soon as she heard someone throwing up in the bathroom.

Sam ran over and found her big sister heaving into the toilet.

"What's the matter?" she asked.

Danni sank to the floor. "I'm either seasick or having the worst case of nerves ever." She struggled to swallow. "My stomach is in knots."

Sam frowned. "What a bummer; I feel great! I love

the motion of the ocean, all the side-to-side and up-and-down—"

"Sam!" Danni cut her off. "Like I'm not queasy enough?"

Sliding down the wall and sitting across from her, Sam bit her lip. "Sorry. Want me to get you some dry toast?"

Danni rubbed her eyes. "No thanks. I need to jump in the shower. We have that fan breakfast thing in forty-five minutes. I don't know how I'm going to make it."

"Olga and I will get there early," Sam offered. "We'll make sure your fans enjoy their breakfast. That way, you don't have to rush."

"Thanks." Danni put a wet rag on her head. "Now, get out and let me barf in peace."

Sam ran over to the second bedroom in the cabin and explained to her sleepy best friend why they had to hurry over to breakfast. The girls got ready and rushed out.

When they reached the ballroom, they found Harley and her manager arguing with a ship's officer. Ducking behind a giant urn, they listened as Harley laid into the poor guy.

"Listen, dude," she snarled, "my manager is right! There is no way you're putting me and my group in the smaller ballroom."

Harley's manager poked his finger into the officer's chest. "You will switch the rooms – *now*."

"But...but...sir," the officer tried to explain, "to exchange rooms at this point would mean changing signs all over the ship! It's impossible to do right now."

"Then you'd better *get to work*!" Harley's manager yelled as he walked away.

Harley nodded. "Dude, get it done." She grabbed the sign that read, *Danni Devine's Fan Breakfast – Ballroom One*, and tore it in half before storming away.

Sam was livid. "That girl is *begging* for a taste of her own medicine," she muttered, as she watched the officer enter a tiny utility room next to what had been Danni's ballroom. A minute later, she saw the same officer use a small key to lock the door, then reach round and stash the key inside a huge potted plant next to the door.

"This could be good." Sam rubbed her hands together like a mad scientist.

Olga had no idea what Sam was planning, but that

didn't stop her from following Sam over to the utility room and watching her snag the hidden key.

"Harley, it's payback time!" said Sam.

"What, with that little key?" Olga asked.

Sam unlocked the door of the utility room. She flipped on a light and walked in. Olga followed her. "Sam, I see brooms and mops and controls for lights and a sound system…and – *wait a minute*!" Olga began to understand. "These controls are for the ballroom next door? The ballroom that *was* Danni's and is now *Harley's*?"

Sam grabbed Olga by the shoulders. "I need you to run back to our cabin and get my iPod and my laptop!"

Olga bolted across the ship in record time. She returned and proudly handed Sam the equipment. While Sam fiddled around, Olga hurried over to Ballroom Two and made sure that Danni's fans were enjoying their breakfast. Once Sam completed her evil plan she snuck out.

"It's all set," Sam whispered to Olga once she slipped into Ballroom Two. "We're twenty minutes from payback!" Sam wanted to gloat more, but Rose, with the camera crew following her, entered the ballroom.

To look innocent, Sam grabbed a basket of fruit and set apples and oranges in front of Danni's fans, whether they wanted them or not.

As she did this, Sam counted down the minutes and got so lost in her thoughts that she didn't notice her mom approaching. She jumped when Rose put her arm round her.

"Sweetie, I think it's wonderful how you and Olga have been holding the fort for your sister," Rose said as she waved to Grandpa Abe across the room. "Why don't you take a break and go sit with your grandfather for a bit?"

Abe waved back enthusiastically and Sam tee-heed with pleasure. She started walking towards him, but then she noticed the time. Harley's payback was set to begin in sixty seconds.

"Hey, Olga!" Sam motioned for her friend. "Would you hang with Grandpa Abe for a minute? I want to sneak over and see how Harley handles our little surprise."

"Sure." Olga nodded. "But you *have* to take some video on your cellphone."

Sam gave a quick thumbs up before slinking away

to the back entrance of Harley's ballroom. She wiggled into a spot behind a curtain; from her vantage point, she had a perfect view of Harley sitting on top of a table, shoving a muffin into her mouth.

Glancing down at her cellphone, Sam noted that she still had twenty-five seconds to wait. She wondered how Harley would react. Would she get all angry? Would she cry?

Harley grabbed a microphone. "You fans are lucky, 'cause in two nights' time, on this very boat, I'm gunna give you *the* best show you've ever seen in your *entire lives!*"

The room erupted with cheers. Sam was disgusted, but then the happy crowd was abruptly drowned out by the theme tune of Barney, every toddler's favourite purple dinosaur, blasting painfully out of the speakers. The fans covered their ears and booed. Harley stood on the table and yelled for somebody to shut off that terrible noise. It was beyond awesome! The event was totally ruined. Downloading the song onto her iPod, and then setting it to play on a timer through the ballroom's sound system had been an inspired idea, Sam thought proudly. Harley's fans whistled and whined. Soon, everybody stormed out of the room.

Sam held up her cellphone, intending to take a video of the whole mess, but then she thought she heard it ringing. She was surprised to see it was Olga calling.

"It worked!" Sam shouted joyfully into the phone. "We totally triumphed!"

"No!" Olga cried. "We totally *tanked*!"

"What? Olga?" Sam didn't realize how loudly she was talking into her handset. "Olga! I can't hear you!"

"That's funny, 'cause I can hear *you* just fine."

As Sam slowly raised her head to find herself getting the evil eye from Harley, her heart sank. She knew she was in a *ton* of trouble.

Harley grabbed a handful of Sam's hair and used it to pull her up and out of the ballroom. Once in the lobby, Sam was surprised to see it so full of people, not just Harley's fans and her scary manager, but Danni, Rose, Robert, Grandpa Abe and all of Danni's fans too. Olga ran over to Sam.

"The music controls you messed with," she whispered, "they weren't just for the *one* ballroom!"

Sam groaned, "Oh, no."

Harley quickly figured out that it was the two

guilty-looking girls who had ruined her fan breakfast. "You two are gunna pay for this!"

Rose rushed over with Danni and Robert close behind; suddenly, Sam and Olga found themselves standing in the middle of a terrible scene. There was hollering and finger-pointing all round. It only ended when Rose ordered everyone to hush and then asked Sam straight out if she had caused this situation. Sam bit her lip and nodded.

Rose banished both Sam and Olga to their cabin – effective *immediately*.

Neither girl spoke as they walked back, knowing full well that they were in detention. Sadly, they both flopped onto their beds.

Abruptly, Sam leaped up and ping-ponged around the cabin. Olga looked concerned, but decided it was best to stay quiet and let whatever was going on, go on. Sam was obsessively plugging in gadgets and wires. Her focus darted back and forth from the computer screen to the clock on the wall.

Five minutes later, Rose was pounding on the cabin door. Sam yelled out, "Be right there, Mom," but instead of rushing over to let her mother into the room,

Sam began frantically unplugging everything she'd just put together.

"Olga," she whispered as she tossed her tiniest MP3 player onto Olga's bed, "hide this!"

Olga caught the digital music player and thrust it under her pillow.

Rose Devine stormed into the cabin and demanded that Sam hand over every piece of technology. Without arguing, Sam gathered up her computer, iPod, Game Boy and PSP. She put them into her special travel case and held it out for confiscation.

"Your cellphone?" Rose asked pointedly

Sam gasped. "My phone? But Mom, I—"

Rose thrust her hand out. "Do not argue, Samanatha Sue. You will relinquish every gidget, gadget and gizmo. I want every toy, every tool – any and everything you've got that needs electricity, be it from the wall or from a battery; fork it over – *now*!"

Sam turned her back on her mom to reach for her cellphone and made eye contact with Olga; she quickly mouthed the word, "*No*". Olga stayed seated on her bed, blocking Mrs. Devine's view of the pillow and the MP3 player hidden beneath it.

Once Sam put her cellphone into the travel case, Rose scooped it up and marched out of the room, pausing only to stare at the TV's remote control. She grabbed that too, shoved it into her pocket, and stormed towards the cabin door. When she reached the doorway to the hall, she spun around.

"Young ladies," she said in a pinched voice, "I am going out to spend a wonderful day at sea. You will not leave this cabin. Your lunch will be brought to you. You will eat it in this cabin. I will return at supper time, dressed for a lovely dinner in the ship's main dining room; you will be waiting for my arrival with the full knowledge that *your* dinner will be delivered to and eaten in this room. When next I step inside this cabin, I expect to see *five* handwritten letters of apology. One letter will be to Harley's fans and the second will be to Danni's, expressing your remorse at ruining their events this morning. The third letter will be to the captain and crew of this fine ship. The last two letters will be your most sincere requests for forgiveness; one goes to Danni, and the other to Harley."

"*What?!*"

Sam knew she was in no position to fight her mom,

but surely Rose *couldn't* be serious. After all the trouble Harley had caused the Devine family, the idea of apologizing to her was *way wrong*. Still, Rose was angry and if the options were to write the letter or live without her computer for ever more, the choice was clear.

"Okay, Mom," she whispered.

Robert's voice bellowed from the hallway. "Rose, we're late for Danni's rehearsal. Lock the brats in their cabin and let's go."

Rose exited the cabin without another word.

As soon as she heard the door close, Sam crumpled to the floor and wailed, "I'm sorry, Olga! I didn't mean to get you into trouble!"

"Oh, please! This is so no-big-deal!" Olga threw herself onto the edge of her bunk and peered over. "Your mom is mad and she's just taking time to calm down. That's *way* better than having her hover."

"I suppose." Sam moped.

"Seriously." Olga reached into her travel bag, pulled out a box of chocolate biscuits from the hotel, and tossed it to Sam. "We should be thankful that all we have to do is write letters. Don't they still punish people at sea by making them walk the plank?"

"Aye, matey," Sam replied in her best pirate voice, "and they might yet make us swab the decks, too!"

This lightened the mood in the cabin. Sam got up and grabbed some paper and a pen; however, she was interrupted by a knock on the cabin door.

Thinking it was already lunchtime, she flung the door open, and was happily surprised to find Grandpa Abe and Red instead.

"I...I can't come out," Sam stammered. "I'm sort of...the truth is..."

"You are *grounding*, yes, your mother explained." Grandpa Abe nodded.

"Yeah, *grounded*. Mom is *really* mad. I'm not allowed out of this cabin."

From behind Sam, Olga's voice rang out, "But she didn't say we couldn't have visitors come into our cabin!"

"That's right!" Sam exclaimed. "Grandpa Abe, would you like to come in?"

Abe hesitated. "A wonderful invitation, yes, but seeing as you share this room with your sister, would it not be better for Red and I to stay out here, in the hallway?"

Sam slapped her forehead. "Duh!" She set a chair outside the door. "How's that?"

Sitting and motioning for Red to lay at his feet, Abe appeared contented. "Nice!"

Sam and Olga grabbed sofa cushions and made themselves equally comfy on the floor. They were careful to stay on the inside of the doorway. The time flew by for Sam. She enjoyed talking and sharing stories with her best friend and her grandfather.

A waiter appeared with a large tray at noon. Rose had ordered way too much food for the girls, so there was plenty to share with Abe and Red. Another wonderful hour slipped by; Sam was shocked to see how fast the day was going. When Rose had said that she was being stripped of her electronics, it sounded like the worst thing in the world. Yet chilling on a pile of cushions in the doorway of her cabin was turning out to be one of the most awesome experiences of the entire trip. Maybe she didn't need so many digital toys. Oh! She remembered something special and ran back inside to her bedroom. She reached under Olga's pillow and grabbed the hidden MP3 player.

"I think you'll enjoy this," Sam said as she handed the tiny audio player to her grandfather.

Sam had to help Abe put the headphones on so he

could hear. As the songs played, it became obvious that he was swept up in the music. Sam saw the change in her grandfather and was thrilled.

Abe pulled off the headphones. "That was unlike anything I ever heard," he said. "It was beautiful, Samantha. You found the song Golda liked so much!"

Sam's voice was full of joy. "I got on my computer and downloaded thirty different versions of 'Pennies from Heaven'. Keep them – the music player and the headphones. I thought you should be able to listen to your Golda's song any time you wanted."

Sam and Olga could see that Grandpa Abe was close to tears. Olga excused herself and slipped inside to the suite's tiny kitchenette to make Abe a cup of tea. Seeing her grandpa so emotional made Sam feel like crying. To lighten the moment, she switched her attention to Red.

"You are such a good boy, aren't you?" Sam scratched Red's tummy. "Yes, you are! Yes, you are! Who is a good boy? Who is the best boy ever?"

"Aw, isn't dat cute, *Chicken Little* making baby talk with da big bad doggie?"

Every muscle in Sam's body tightened as she cringed

in embarrassment. She raised her head and was mortified to see Harley and her manager totally laughing at her.

Great, Sam thought. *Hasn't this day had enough drama already?*

Just then, Michi and Lou appeared in the hall and started taping the scene. Sam shook her head and sighed.

CHAPTER 17

"I heard your *mommy* grounded you," Harley snarled at Sam. "Think she'd be cool with you hanging in the hallway like this?"

Red, who had been resting at Abe's feet, sprang up, bared his teeth, and let out a deep, dark growl. Harley pulled her arm back, but otherwise remained frozen.

"*Przestać*, Red," Abe said sternly to the dog. "*Przestać*. All is good." Immediately the dog relaxed and returned to his previous position at his master's feet. Abe gazed up at Harley. "I am very sorry, Miss. Please excuse Mr. Red. He does not mean harm to you; he was thinking only of protecting our young

Samantha. I know this is the second time he has shown you his teeth. I give you my promise that it will not happen again. I hope you can forgive an old dog." Abe gently smiled. "And Red, too."

Harley studied Abe's face for some clue as to why he was being such a gentleman. Sam felt as if she could read what was going on in Harley's brain: wondering if the old man's acting-polite deal was for real or some kind of put-on.

"Um, well…' Harley was tongue-tied. "I *guess* I can understand. He musta thought I was gunna backhand the kid."

"I am *not* a kid," Sam shot back, "and you're old enough to know that 'gunna' isn't even a word. You were 'going' to backhand me: '*going*', not '*gunna*'." She rolled her eyes. "*Everybody* knows that!"

Grandpa Abe struggled to stand as he cleared his throat to get attention. "Miss Harley, I recognize that *we* are taking up your time. For Red, Samantha and myself, please accept that this rude behaviour is now over. Do not let us take up any more of your day." He bowed his head. "Please accept our apology for interrupting your afternoon."

Harley's manager stepped out from behind his client. "Nice try, Gramps, but you can take your apology and—"

He didn't finish his sentence because Harley stomped on his toe. She gave Abe a tiny nod and headed back down the hallway. Her manager raced to catch up.

Olga stepped into the doorway with the tea for Abe and was surprised to find him standing and Sam looking puzzled. "Here we go," she said as she set down the tray. "I'm pretty beat, so I'm going back in for a nap. See you later."

"Grandpa Abe?" Sam asked softly. "I don't understand why you said what you said to Harley. It sounded like you were apologizing to her for *me*."

Abe took in a slow breath before answering. "Samantha, I have not been your grandfather for long; it would not be my place to admonish your behaviour. However, I will ask: do you feel your comments to Miss Harley were justified?"

"J-J-Justified?" Sam stuttered. "You mean *fair*? Was *I fair* to Harley? I don't know. Maybe…" She thought for a moment. "Um, maybe not…but, Grandpa Abe, you do not know how many terrible things she's said about Danni!"

Abe chose his words carefully. "Is this need for fairness what is most important to you? You can worry about everything and everyone being fair or you can forget fair and think more about what kind of person you want to be. Me? I choose to behave as a good person; this means I usually *am* a good person. No one is perfect, and sometimes I am not in the mood to be *friendly*, but I can always be polite. Another's rudeness often is because of their own problems; issues that are not related to me. If you decide always to act in a manner you can take pride in, eventually the world sees that pride and admires it and becomes nicer to you in return. It is up to you – if you rush to sneer at everyone you think has been rude, soon everyone will be sneering at you, and that is no good." He sighed. "Do you know why that is no good?"

Sam shook her head. She didn't want to say anything stupid just as her grandfather was sharing his wisest thoughts with her.

"Sneering is no good because it gives you the pimples."

Nodding, Sam mulled over Abe's wise words, but then it hit her – *pimples*? His valuable life lesson was about zits? She looked up at her grandfather. "...*Pimples?*"

Abe let out a great belly guffaw. It was the most genuine laughter Sam had ever heard and it filled her with joy. Oh! He'd made a *joke*!

"I wanted to be sure you were paying attention," Abe said as he leaned down and patted Sam on the head. "You are a good girl, Samantha. You have a good heart. Don't let another with their own set of problems take away the goodness inside you."

Abe motioned towards his chair. "You can take that back inside. I will go to the kennels with Red. We both need a rest. You have letters to write, yes?"

"I almost forgot!" Sam slapped her forehead. "I'm supposed to write five different apologies. I have to get them done or I'm going be one dead duck."

"Get to work, young lady," Abe called out over his shoulder as he and Red walked away, "I am a good veterinarian, but once the duck is dead, there is little I can do."

Sam pulled Abe's chair back into the cabin.

Standing alone in the doorway, she remembered that she wasn't really alone. Looking further down the hallway, she spied Michi and Lou, still standing there, videotaping away.

"Hey, Michi," she called out. "May I borrow your earpiece to speak to Blu?"

Michi pressed on her earpiece. "What? Okay." She looked into Sam's eyes. "Blu says no, quit being a goofus and go write your apology letters – *now*."

Sam rolled her eyes. "*I'm going, I'm going.*" She closed the cabin door and yelled loudly enough for Michi and Lou to hear, "I'm gone!"

Then she took off running into her room, took a flying leap, and yelled out, "Cowabunga," as she did a bellyflop onto her bed.

"Freakshow," Olga yelled out as she threw a pillow at Sam. "You made me ruin my last letter."

"Your *last* letter?" Sam groaned. "If I only had my computer! By hand, this is going to take me for ever."

Rose's voice floated into the bedroom.

"Girls?" she called out as she knocked on the cabin door. "It's time. I'm here with your sister and we would both like to see your letters."

Sam cringed. "*Great!* Now Mom really *is* going to ground me for the rest of my life! It's been nice knowing you, Olga. I'll miss you."

Olga handed Sam several sheets of paper and a pen. "Run into the bathroom and sign these while I keep your mom occupied."

It took Sam a moment to understand that in her hand she was holding five beautifully written letters of apology. "I can't take your letters!"

"Yes, you can," Olga hissed as she closed the bedroom door behind her and went to deal with Mrs. Devine and Danni in the living room of the suite. "Your mom can't ground *me* for ever. I'll be fine."

While Olga kept Rose occupied, Sam sank onto the bedroom floor and quickly read the letters. They were amazing, and *before* her conversation with Grandpa Abe, these would have been exactly the kind of letters Sam would have written. However, Grandpa Abe's words about choosing how to act and taking pride in her behaviour had really sunk in; Sam wanted those ideas to show in her letters. She grabbed a pen and a single sheet of paper and wrote out her letter to Harley. Then she darted out to where Olga, Rose and Danni were waiting.

"Mom." Sam approached with the letter out in front of her. "Olga's letters are all done. I only completed one letter, and I *super-double-promise* I'll get the other four done before dinner, but I want you to read this before you get mad at me."

Rose reached for the paper. As she read it, her expression changed from one of way sceptical to total approval.

"Little Bit…" Rose smiled proudly. "This letter… it's *beautiful*; so beautiful, in fact, there's a chance Harley might actually accept your apology." Rose got up from the sofa. "I will be back in one hour for you to show me the rest of your handiwork." As she exited the cabin, Rose whipped back round. "Believe me, Samantha Sue, it is *only* because that letter is *so outstanding* that you're getting this extra time to finish the others."

Sam didn't waste a second. She sat down and wrote out her other four letters. It didn't take the full hour, but she couldn't leave yet. Rose had to approve these letters before she was officially *sprung from jail*. Without any electronics to play with, Sam was big-time bored. She paced around the suite several times before wandering into Danni's bedroom.

"Danni?"

There was no movement or sound from her sister, who was lying face down on her bed, with her head in her pillow.

Sam tried again, a tad louder. "Hey, Danni?"

Still no movement, but Danni did mumble back, "Mmmm?"

Sam sat on the foot of her sister's bed. "Danni? Are you sleeping?"

Danni rolled over onto her back. "Uh…not any more." She stared up at the ceiling.

"I'm really sorry about today. Are you okay?" Sam asked.

"Yeah," she replied softly. "I'm fine. I'm perfect. I'm peachy-keen."

Sam lay down, curling around Danni's feet and asked, "You aren't worried about the concert, are you?" She sat back up and looked at her sister. "You can't be thinking that there is any chance that you aren't going to knock everybody's socks off and prove to the whole world that Harley is nothing but a big ole poser, right?"

Danni put her arms up to her head to cover her eyes. "I don't want to talk about it."

"You *have* to know how amazing you are," Sam said in her most serious voice. "How could you go from doing dinky little beauty pageants to being adored by folks all over the planet if you weren't such a special talent? I'm *always* amazed when you sing and such beautiful sounds come out. Where *did* you get such talent? Not from Mom, that's for sure! And we all know *I* can't sing. Oh!" Sam remembered something Abe had said. "It's from Golda! Remember? Grandpa Abe talked about her being his songbird! He said her singing was *magic*; well that's what it is when you sing, Danni – magic! Forget all the costumes and dance numbers. Just plain old you and your singing – it's magical."

Danni remained motionless, with her arms still covering her eyes, but Sam caught sight of a tear running down her cheek.

"Little Bit," she snuffled, "go to my suitcase, the big one in my closet. There's a box hidden underneath a bunch of T-shirts. Grab it for me, will ya?"

"Happy to." Sam returned with the box. "Your package, my lady."

Danni raised herself up on her elbows. "Now, I

 241

need you to go to your room, close the door, and open the box. Whatever you do, don't let Mom see what's in that box – at least, not yet."

Confused, Sam asked, "You want me to what? And not tell Mom what? *What?*"

Danni lay back down and returned to staring up at the ceiling. "I got you something special in London. Just go!"

Sam skedaddled back to her and Olga's bedroom. She carefully placed the package on her bed and gingerly lifted the lid off the box. Inside she found a folded note with her name on it, sitting on top of a parcel wrapped in tissue paper. She opened the note and read it out loud.

"'Dear Sam, I know your thirteenth birthday is just around the corner, but I' – *Hey!*" Sam's jaw dropped as a jolt of "duh" zapped her brain. "*It is!* My thirteenth birthday *is* just around the corner! Olga!" Sam looked up at her best friend. "I've been so nuts with this trip and Grandpa Abe and Harley that I *forgot* that I'll be a real live thirteen-year-old in just two weeks! Is that not *the* most mental thing *ever?*"

Olga thought before answering, "It is pretty

demented. Still –" her eyes focused back on the box – "keep reading!"

Sam returned to the letter. "'I know your thirteenth birthday is just around the corner, but I wanted to give you this special present a little bit early – or should I say a *Little Bit* early – as my way of not just celebrating you becoming a teenager, but also thanking you for always supporting me. You are the best little sister a gal could ever have, and I love you more than french fries love ketchup! Happy thirteenth birthday (early). Love, Danni'."

Moving cautiously, Sam pulled back the tissue paper. Several layers of blue paper protected whatever it was in the middle of the box, until she reached a single layer of white tissue. When she pulled that back, she finally got to see her gift. She slammed her hands over her mouth to stop herself from screaming.

Click click click, clack clack click.

SCHMOOZE CRUISE – DAY #2

I have THE MOST ROCKING sister in the whole

wide world!! Danni just gave me the *most gorgeous, brand-new, itty-bitty laptop* for my birthday – early – but that makes it even cooler! I have so much to write, but I have to do it super fast. Technically, I'm grounded from ALL technology – so if my mom catches me blogging on this *most gorgeous, brand-new, itty-bitty laptop,* she'll take it away. Now – my blog:

After I opened the box and discovered this *most gorgeous, brand-new, itty-bitty laptop*, I ran back into Danni's room to thank her. As I was showering my big sis with gratitude, I had a moment of genius. See, Danni was worried about not being spectacular enough in her showdown with Harley. She was doubting herself and her talent.

My idea was to do a totally different kind of song, something beautiful that would let her show off her sensational singing ability, a song nobody would be expecting – Grandma Golda's song – "Pennies From Heaven"!

At first Danni wasn't too hot on the idea, but after I explained what a great surprise it would be for Grandpa Abe and played her three different versions that I'd downloaded to my *most gorgeous, brand-new, itty-bitty laptop,* she "got it". Right now, she's on a conference call with her band. They are working on the perfect pop version of the tune; by the time everyone gets flown in tomorrow for rehearsals, the song should be ready to go!

My mom should be here soon to read all of my apology letters from this prank Olga and I pulled this morning (it turned out seriously bad – don't ask!). I hope she hurries. As soon as I'm released from "jail", I'm heading down to the kennels to hang with Grandpa Abe and Red, but I won't stay too late. Tomorrow is our last full day at sea before we reach New York and there are a million things to do. For a start, I'm going to do EVERYTHING I can to make sure that...

#1 – Grandpa Abe and Red get the best seats

for the concert so they can see how amazingly talented Danni truly is;

#2 – Danni's big rehearsal tomorrow goes well so she's ready to take on Harley at the concert;

#3 – I *finally* get an answer from Grandpa Abe about why his so-not-red dog is named *Red*.

TTFN!

CHAPTER 18

Sam was totally zonked out when the ringing of the phone next to her head woke her up. With her eyes closed, she tried to put the receiver to her ear, but ended up bonking herself in the middle of her forehead.

"Ouch!" Her eyes shot wide open.

"Good morning, Little Bit," came the cheery response. "Rise and shine! Devine family breakfast meeting in my cabin in exactly ten minutes. Tomorrow is Danni's concert and we have a million details to discuss."

Sam let her eyes close as she murmured, "Yes, Mother."

"*Samantha Sue!*" Rose hollered into the phone. "Get yourself *out* of that bed and *into* that shower, *now!*"

Nine-and-a-half minutes later, Sam and Olga raced into Rose's cabin.

"Nice to see you, ladies." Rose smiled as she closed the cabin door behind them. "Grab something to eat from the buffet there and sit. We have no time to waste today."

Sam saw Robert and Danni enjoying their breakfast. She snagged a muffin and looked around.

"Mom," she asked, "are we going to wait for Grandpa Abe?"

Rose shook her head. "No, Sweetie. He needs to rest. This is a long trip for an old man. You'll be – wait a minute – *Robert*—" She waved her napkin at him. "Please explain."

Robert stood and handed two long sheets of yellow paper to each person. Sam's eyes almost popped out of her head as she tried to read all the teeny-tiny print. Every single minute between that morning's breakfast and the concert the following evening had been mapped out. A chart showed which person had been

put in charge of each task; most of the work had been placed on Robert's shoulders.

In spite of everything she'd learned from all of her past experiences with him, Sam found herself having to admit that the big lug really had done an amazing job of making sure everything was taken care of. *He put a ton of thought and hard work into this and made it appear so easy,* she thought. *If Mom had had to do this on her own, the workload would have been brutal.*

"Hey!" Robert's voice jarred Sam. He was standing in front of her, waving an envelope. "Did you hear what I said about making sure Abe understands that I was able to get clearance for him and Red to stay in the United States for up to thirty days, as long as I get his signature on these papers *today*? This isn't a joke; I have to fax these forms this afternoon. Can you handle it?"

Genuinely pleased that Robert was taking care of her grandfather, Sam nodded. "Get you the signed forms super-soon, check."

"And Danni…" Robert turned his back on Sam so he could focus. "You don't need to worry, I've made sure that the hotel down the block from your house has a suite for Abe and Red. They will be close enough to visit, but the dog *won't* be staying in the house."

Danni sighed gratefully. "That's awesome, Robert. Thank you."

Sam caught Robert sneaking a glance at Rose. *He's trying to impress her!* she thought. *He's hoping she'll see that we really do need him in our crazy lives!*

"Sam and Olga." Robert span back around to face the two girls. "Tomorrow afternoon, the dog *must* be bathed, brushed and buckled into his travel harness by four o'clock so that when the ship's officer comes to escort you up to the VIP seats, you won't throw him off *his* schedule. Are we clear?"

Both girls nodded.

"I had to pull serious strings with the captain to get permission for that dog to be allowed on deck for the show," Robert continued. "We cannot afford the smallest slip-up or Red will have to leave, and you know as well as I do that Abe won't stay anywhere without his dog."

Sam caught Robert stealing another quick glance at Rose.

"Mr. Ruebens," Rose said, without making eye

contact with him, "you appear to have things under control." And just like that, she walked out.

Sam couldn't believe what she saw next. Rose's cold behaviour seemed to physically hurt Robert. His shoulders slouched. His painfully bright smile vanished. It was obvious that Robert was sad; even Danni saw it. She patted him on the back.

"Honestly, Robert," she said, "it's a miracle the way you pulled so much together for me – for our whole family – in such a short period of time. Thanks for everything."

Danni walked to the door and yelled, "Hang on, Mom. My schedule says that my band and dancers are being helicoptered here to the ship in about five minutes and I need to get right to work with them. Why don't you come with me?" She turned back into the cabin. "See you at lunch, Robert?"

He nodded half-heartedly.

Danni left. Sam and Olga found themselves alone in the cabin with a sullen, silent Robert. Neither girl knew what to do; they kept looking back and forth from each other to their gloomy companion. Finally, Sam decided to put her grandfather's advice to the test.

She grabbed a chair and plopped herself down in front of Robert. "All right, you don't like me and I don't like you, but I have to admit that for all your jerkiness, you've always done *exactly* what you said you would – taken great care of my sister's career and made us a ton of money. If my mom had to deal with all the crazy details that you do, her head would explode."

A tiny smirk crept across Robert's face.

"Here's what I don't understand." Sam shook her head. "You're scary-successful. You're not completely hideous-looking, and you're not too old to get a life; *why* are you still making a big deal of hanging out with my family? My mom *fired* you. You should be thinking about taking care of your other clients, or finding *new* clients, or buying a sports car – doing whatever guys do when they get down."

"I'm not *down*," Robert snapped. "I'm powerful and wealthy. I'm never *down*."

Sam shrugged. "Okay, if that's how you want it. Olga, let's go see if Grandpa Abe and Red would like to go walk around the deck."

"Wait," Robert called out. "What are you up to?"

"I am not 'up to' anything," Sam groaned, before

explaining to him all the amazing advice and ideas Abe had shared with her the day before.

Sitting back in his chair, Robert asked, "But what do you want from *me*?"

Sam jumped to her feet and stared at him eye-to-eye. "I want you to stop being a phoney-baloney who upsets my mom. I want you to keep taking care of the details of my sister's career so my mom and my sister can be happy, because I'm afraid that once you really are out of the picture it'll be too much for my *mom*, and she'll freak out, and that will make my *sister* get stressed, and then *nobody* will be happy – ever again!"

Robert studied her suspiciously. "Let's say I agree to, as you put it, 'stop being a phoney-baloney', what good would it do? Your mother has made it clear that when Danni's concert is over, my job with your family is *finished*."

Sam caught Olga's eye. The two girls exchanged the kind of silent communication that only best friends can. Olga walked over to Sam. Both girls folded their arms as they stood shoulder-to-shoulder.

"Honestly, Robert," Sam spoke matter-of-factly, "for a smart dude, sometimes you are dense as a forest. Have

you not yet figured out that when Olga and I put our heads together, there's nothing we can't accomplish?"

Robert stood to escape. "I'm walking away from this conversation before it gets any weirder." He strode out of the cabin.

Sam scratched her head. "I think he just agreed to our deal. Yes? I mean, he didn't tell us *not* to try and get his job back, right?"

"Absolutely! He totally gave you the green light," Olga gushed. "Nice work, Sam."

With a pleased little curtsy, Sam replied, "Thank you very much."

Olga sat on the arm of the sofa. "So what *is* your plan?"

"No idea," Sam answered as she plopped down on the other armrest. "You?"

Olga shook her head. "I got nothing."

Click click click, clack clack click.

SCHMOOZE CRUISE – DAY #3

Olga and I spent the morning trying to figure out

how to keep my end of a deal I made with Robert (don't ask – just go with me on this).

In the middle of working on our plan, we noticed we were late for Danni's rehearsal. We snuck (or is it sneaked) we sneaked in a side door; no one noticed us (whew).

The rehearsal was off-the-charts! Danni's new dance song is going to be a mega hit; you can't hear it without tapping your feet.

Then Danni tried out her big closing number. I kind of freaked because I thought she'd changed her mind and wasn't going to sing the Grandpa Abe/Grandma Golda song; turns out I was *way wrong*. Standing alone in the middle of the stage, Danni sang softly at first, but then really put her heart into it and sang "Pennies From Heaven" better than I'd ever heard her sing anything – EVER! The whole room was spellbound and – get this – I saw *Harley* hiding at the back. She got all choked up and had to

bite her bottom lip to stop it from quivering! *For real!*

My gut reaction was to tell Harley that she was right to be all emotional because there was NOTHING she could sing at the concert that would be half as good as that song, but my dedication to Grandpa Abe's advice is real – so I zipped it and stayed where I was – *until* I noticed Harley's manager whispering into Harley's ear. Whatever he said made Harley laugh. That made me so mad I thought I was going to explode! I stomped towards them.

But before I could get close, Robert walked over and told Harley and her manager that he was glad to have them at the rehearsal. He wanted Harley to see for herself why she needed to be prepared to be "put to shame in the talent department" at the concert tomorrow. Harley froze like a popsicle. She had no idea how to answer that. Her manager, however, totally lost his temper and stormed out of the ballroom.

Seeing Harley there all alone, she seemed rather sad to me – I almost felt sorry for her...ALMOST!

I need to end this blog. Olga and me are supposed to be in the dining room right now; it's time to activate our plan to get Robert his job back!

I promise to share all the details as soon as I can!

Even though the main dining room, with its huge crystal chandeliers, was dazzling, Sam wished her mom had let them eat dinner in their cabin, where they wouldn't have had to dress up. Her pointy shoes were killing her feet and the dress didn't fit properly. Plus, the fact that Grandpa Abe was late for dinner bothered her. *Be cool*, she told herself, *you have to stay focused. You have an important mission tonight.*

Rose was in a great mood. She beamed when the ship's captain stopped by to say hello to her. *This is good*, Sam thought. *The happier she is now, the more open she'll be to what Olga and I have to say.*

Danni, followed by Michi and Lou, joined the table with a pile of papers she was studying furiously.

"Robert gave me tons of rehearsal notes. Please excuse me from family talk tonight."

Rose patted her elder daughter's arm. "I'm proud of you, Honey. Do what you have to do. We understand." Rose turned to gaze at Sam and Olga. "Don't we, ladies?"

Both girls nodded. Danni shot them a grateful grin and went back to cramming.

Robert entered the dining room with his head held high. He sat in between Rose and Sam, and, as usual, ignored Sam's presence.

"You both look beautiful this evening," he said to Rose and Danni as he put his napkin on his lap. "I'm honoured to be joining you for our last dinner at sea."

"That's right!" Sam exclaimed. "We're in New York tomorrow!" She turned to Olga. "My, but this trip has gone by quickly, wouldn't you say, *Olga*?"

Playing along, Olga nodded. "Yes, Sam! This entire trip has zoomed by."

Sam clasped her hands. "Yes, it has zoomed by. Why do you think that is, Olga?"

Olga furrowed her brow. "Well, maybe it is like the old saying, *time flies when you're having fun.*"

 258

"*Time flies when you're having fun,*" Sam repeated. "Hmm. I would have to agree with you on that, Olga. Time *does* fly by when you are enjoying yourself. Which is rather amazing when you consider how many eenie-beanie details had to be handled in a seriously brief period of time for us to fly to another country, meet a long-lost grandfather, get to enjoy a first-class Atlantic crossing on our way home, and then settle this whole Harley issue by going head-to-head with her in a once-in-a-lifetime concert in front of the whole world."

Sam was rather pleased. So far, everything she and Olga had practised was sounding really good. However, she lost that positive vibe when she looked up and saw Rose, Robert and Danni all staring at her with scepticism.

Olga continued playing her part. "Boy oh boy, Sam, you sure are right about that. I cannot even begin to imagine what a nightmare it must have been to get all the plane tickets and limousines and hotel rooms organized for us! And then, to hear that everything has been cleared so your Grandpa Abe and his dog can stay in the United States for a couple of weeks' vacation with you and your family! However did your family manage to put all of this together? You must have had some amazing assistance, because this all sounds too good to be true!"

"Yes," Rose growled softly, "it *is* too good to be true." Staring into her daughter's eyes, Rose asked, "Samantha Sue, what's going on here?"

Sam tried to avoid her mom's steely gaze by grabbing a pitcher and filling her water glass. "Nothing. Olga and I are just making dinner conversation. Right, Olga?"

Olga forced a smile and nodded.

Rose drilled more. "Since when have you girls made dinner conversation about *details*?"

Sam and Olga both lowered their heads. Then Sam glanced over at Robert to see if he recognized that she was failing in her attempt to help him.

When Rose saw this, she drummed her fingers on the table. Her head swivelled back and forth; she looked at Robert and back at Sam several times. Finally, Rose stood up. "Robert Ruebens," she hissed, "you've pulled some schemes before, but to use *two innocent children* to trick me into rehiring you? That is

low, very low – that's lower than a snake's stomach!"

Oh no, Sam thought, *Mom thinks Robert put us up to this!* She felt terrible! She knew she should explain to her mom that this wasn't Robert's doing, that it was completely her own idea. She tried to interrupt, but her mom was way too focused on Robert to even notice Sam.

Whipping round on her dangerously high heels, Rose teetered, before steadying herself against the table. Robert instinctively put his arm out to help, but Rose pulled away, smoothed her hair, and stormed out of the dining room.

Utterly lost, Danni asked, "Could somebody please explain to me what just happened?" She rubbed her temples. "Never mind. Don't tell me *anything*. I'm going to take a bubble bath and order room service and go to sleep." She scurried out.

The three bodies left at the table sat stone-faced. Finally Sam slapped her hand down on the table. "I can fix this," she said. "Trust me, Robert, I can *totally* fix this."

Robert kept his eyes focused on the table. "I'm going for a walk. Maybe the cool ocean air will clear my head and help me forget that a twelve-year-old girl managed to shred the last bit of respect I had from my top client...*former* top client."

Sam tried to apologize, but Robert waved her off. "Forget it. It is what it is. I'm done. I have plenty of other clients I should be taking care of; your family has been ridiculously high-maintenance. I'll be seeing... I..." Robert got up and left.

The waiter came to the table. "Good evening, ladies." He set down menus. "Would you like a soft drink before your meal?"

Sam shook her head. Olga handed the menus back to the waiter.

"Thanks," she said, "but we've lost our appetites."

The girls slowly rose from the table and trudged sadly back to their cabin. Neither one spoke.

It wasn't until they reached their cabin door and Sam pulled her key out of her pocket that a thought whacked her in the side of the head.

"Wait!" she cried out. "Grandpa Abe never showed up for dinner!"

Olga's hands flew to her mouth as she exclaimed, "Yikes!"

"*Major* yikes!" Sam agreed. "We have to find him and make sure he's okay!"

As they hustled over to Abe's cabin, Olga tried to reassure her friend. "I wouldn't worry, Sam. I'm sure he's fine. He probably just lost track of time."

With a tremor in her voice, Sam responded, "You know, any other time, I'd probably agree with you, but after the way *everything* has gone *so wrong* tonight, I'm having a tough time thinking positive."

That was the last thing either girl said for a while. They tried to act calm as they scooted across the ship, but on the inside, each one was completely freaking out.

CHAPTER 19

After pounding on Grandpa Abe's cabin door and getting no response, Sam and Olga sprinted to the kennels. Neither one spoke.

As they got close, they heard an elderly man's voice. Majorly relieved, the girls slowed down. Sam was about to step through the propped-open kennel door, but Olga reached out and stopped her; then she signalled Sam to be quiet, listen, and join her, as she scrunched over to the side of the door frame. Sam nodded and joined her friend.

"Could you not be getting ahead of yourself?" Grandpa Abe asked whoever was with him. "Could this not be a misunderstanding that needs only a little sunlight to clear it up?"

"Abe, Rose made it clear tonight that there is no chance of her trusting me again."

Sam's eyes flew open so wide they looked like two fried eggs. "That's *Robert!*" she whispered. "What's he doing with *my* grandpa?"

Olga shushed her.

Gritting her teeth, Sam pressed against the door frame to hear better.

"But everyone sometimes missteps. No one person can always be perfect."

"It's time I moved on," Robert griped. "I've given the Devines too much. I've lost other clients because I wasted too much time explaining my business deals to Rose, or calming Danni before a performance, or arranging some surprise for the kid."

Before Sam could start bellyaching about being called "the kid", Olga grabbed her, pushed her behind the massive urn next to the kennel door, and shushed her again.

Sam had no idea why her best friend was acting so oddly, until she heard the familiar clicking noise of

Rose's high heels tromping down the hallway. Even though nothing was funny, Sam had to bite her hand to stop nervous giggles from escaping.

The clicking noise stopped for a moment a little way down the hallway. Sam heard her mom ask somebody if they'd seen an elderly gentleman in the kennels recently. *She must have been worried about Grandpa Abe too,* Sam thought. *That's so cool that, as mad as she was at Robert, Mom cares enough about Grandpa Abe to come check on him.* Her thoughts were interrupted by the clicking sound resuming and growing louder until Rose approached the kennel door. She did exactly what her daughter had done minutes before: she prepared to walk through the open doorway, but stopped when she heard Grandpa Abe's voice.

"You can look *me* in the eye and say you know of mistakes that you would not make again." Grandpa Abe spoke gently. "Why can you not do the same with the Devines? It is plain to see that you care about them."

"Of course I *care*," Robert retorted. "A good agent *has* to care about his clients. It's in the job description: *a good agent must always care.*"

Upon hearing this, Rose put her hands on her hips and tapped her toe.

Oh, Robert, Sam thought, *I'll never be able to fix this if you dig your own grave with that snotty attitude.*

There was amusement in Grandpa Abe's voice. "And who are you fooling with this important business talk? Not *me*. I hear the falseness of your words."

Rose took a tiny step forward and cupped her hand around her ear. It seemed as if she was working extra hard to hear every single syllable coming from the back of the kennel.

Robert sighed. "There's no point in discussing this any more, Abe. Even if I walked up to Rose tonight and admitted all my mistakes; even if I promised her that from this moment on I would only deal in the truth, the whole truth, and nothing but the truth with her, Danni, and even the kid—"

Abe interrupted him. "The kid...?"

"Sam." Robert nodded. "She hates it when I call her *kid*, but I can't help myself." His voice perked up. "Between you and me, it's quite entertaining to watch the steam come out of her ears when I do it."

The two men shared a good-natured chuckle.

Robert continued. "And here's what gets me... I know that the kid, *Sam*, is turning thirteen this month. I shouldn't know that, but I do, because I've wasted a ridiculous amount of time helping Rose plan a birthday surprise for her."

Sam had no idea anybody was planning anything for her birthday! She gasped, but Olga shot her a look that reminded her to remain quiet. Still – a big surprise – for *her*!

"Robert, please," Abe replied. "If you are unhappy doing such things, why have you stayed? You have all the money a man could need. Why put yourself through such unnecessary difficulties?"

Rose, Sam and Olga all strained their ears to get every word of Robert's answer.

"It's been...*different* working with Rose and Danni." Robert spoke slowly. "With my other clients it's easy – it's all business all the time. I'm only needed to handle contracts or negotiations. With Danni, she was such a sweet teenager when we began that I felt protective. Maybe it grew out of her not having a father around, or maybe because Rose seemed truly to value my advice on all matters, not just business. I came to feel like a genuine part of something *real*. The Devines may drive me to the borderline of madness, but they give me a sense of belonging. That doesn't sound too weak, does it?"

Sam sneaked a peek to see how her mom was reacting. Rose had an odd expression on her face – a funny blend of appreciation and exhaustion. Sam ducked back down behind the urn.

"If you want an old man's advice –" it sounded as if Abe had given Robert a friendly slap on the back – "Mr. Ruebens, stand tall and give an apology to the family. Let go of your ego. Tell Rose you will be more open and want to move forward."

Robert sighed before replying. "You make it sound so easy."

Abe grunted. Sam recognized it as the noise he made when he stood up. "Trust me," he said, "it is easy once you decide. The *decision* part, *that* is the most challenging."

The voices of the two men grew louder as they approached the entrance to the kennels.

"I hear you, Abe," said Robert.

Olga pushed back against Sam and whispered, "They're coming out! Squish back a little more!"

Without looking behind her, Sam tried, but found it impossible to scooch more than a millimetre. There seemed to be something behind her. She stretched a hand back, while still looking in the direction of the kennel door, and was surprised to feel something warm – warm and *alive*! Whipping her head round, Sam found herself staring into the very unamused face of her mother.

Click click click, clack clack click.

SCHMOOZE CRUISE – DAY #4

It's 8.45 in the a.m. and I'm typing this from the bathroom of my cabin – yup, still on the ship. This is our last day! We should be pulling into New York Harbour in a couple of hours. Oh! That means I should be packing and then watching out for the Statue of Liberty! But first, I have some amazing stuff to share.

Last night, Olga and I overheard Robert 'fessing up to Grandpa Abe about wanting to change and be a more trustworthy kind of guy with my mom.

I was surprised by this, but Mom (who was eavesdropping as well) was even more so! Her face went so totally blank that she looked like a crashed computer (LOL).

After thinking about what she'd heard (and staying hidden until Robert and Grandpa Abe had left), Mom walked Olga and me to our cabin, gave me a kiss on the cheek, and told us to order some room service and then get to sleep. Then she left. Seriously! THAT WAS IT! No drama, no lecture, *no problem*!

Right now I'm dying inside because I *desperately* want to know what Mom is thinking about Robert. She's tough; once my mom has made a decision, it's almost impossible to get her to change her mind. But she was acting super-strange after overhearing Robert, so right now, I'm not certain of *anything*.

Just checked the clock and now it's 9.10 a.m. As soon as I finish this blog, I'm going to wake Olga

 271

and then we won't have a chance to catch our breath until after Danni's big concert here on the ship – live from New York Harbour – tonight. We're in charge of Grandpa Abe and it's our responsibility to make sure that Red is bathed and in his harness or he can't come up for the show. This is crucial because if Red can't come to the show, then Grandpa Abe won't want to come, and then he'll miss seeing Danni and the whole surprise of the special song will be ruined.

Part of me feels guilty that we aren't directly helping Danni today. She has to be feeling all kinds of pressure; it's her first *live* televised concert, and she has to do it as a showdown against Harley! But my sister *is* a lot like our mom; she's *way* tougher than she looks. My plan for the day is to be sure that no matter what, I will not add to any of Danni's stress. Olga and I will take awesome care of Grandpa and Red. We will get them prepared and fed and to the concert on time. Yup, my prime directive for the day is not to cause my mom or sister any grief.

Ciao for now!!

Breakfast was craziness a gogo. Sam and Olga chomped their way through the buffet in the main dining room, while chaos went on all around them. Helicopters flew in, dropped off people and equipment, and immediately took off to get more stuff. Rose race-walked over to a table, with two men who looked totally identical – except for the fact that one was dressed all in brown and the other all in black – following closely behind her.

"Oh, Jean and Jehan," she panted, "thank goodness you're here!"

The man in the brown clothes gave out a totally fake laugh. "Oh, Roze," he said in a French accent thicker than the maple syrup on Sam's pancakes, "zat lipstick you are wearing is so fabulous, eet eez *to die for!*"

Sam let out a little snort. *Good old Jean,* she thought. *He may be Danni's hair and make-up artist, but his real talent is being a suck-up artist.*

The man dressed all in black nodded intensely. "Zees is true, Roze," he agreed in the same heavy accent.

"However, I sink zat eet eez your perfect pink jumper zat eez what makes you glow like a firefly."

Sam nearly choked on her juice. *Trust Jehan to try to one-up his twin with a comment about Mom's wardrobe,* she thought. *Those two will never, ever change.*

Rose coyly waved a hand. "And that's why you boys are such crucial members of Danni's entourage. Not only are you talented, but you do know how to flatter a gal."

Danni, wearing a baseball cap and dark sunglasses, scooted into the dining room and slumped into a chair. Jean and Jehan showered her with air-kisses and compliments. Both brothers buzzed with excitement about how much press coverage the concert was getting from newspapers, websites and television shows around the world.

Danni listened intently before her eyes welled up with tears. "Oh, Jean, oh, Jehan," she whispered, "I thank my lucky stars you're here."

Rose patted Danni's shoulder. "Sweetheart, we're *all* here for you." Rose looked up. "Okay everyone, today will be crazy. Make sure you get plenty from the buffet."

"No, please," Danni begged. "Don't everyone abandon me. Everywhere I look, I see Harley's fans and Harley's entourage and Harley's manager, and—"

"*Harley!* Good morning, Harley." Sam jumped up and stood in front of her sister to block Harley's view of an unhinged Danni.

Harley ignored Sam as she strode past the table on her way to the buffet. Sam scooted around to ensure that Harley couldn't get a glimpse of her sister. Olga hopped up and stood side-by-side with Sam. After piling her plate with a mound of food, Harley skulked off to the opposite end of the dining room.

"Young ladies, that was positively brilliant," came Abe's proud voice from behind the girls. They both turned to see him standing at the table with a huge grin on his face. Robert pulled out a chair for him.

"Have a seat, Abe," he said. "I'll get breakfast for both of us."

Rose introduced Abe to Jean and Jehan. Sam was impressed that her grandpa remembered which one was which right away. Even after having them around for an entire year, Sam was forever mixing up the twins.

 275

Robert returned with two plates of food. He carefully placed one in front of Abe before glancing over and realizing that neither Rose nor Danni had anything.

"Rose, Danni," he asked politely, "would either one of you like this plate, or may I get one for you?"

Danni shook her head. "No, thanks. *So* not hungry."

Rose nodded. "I'll take you up on that offer, Mr. Ruebens."

Robert set his plate in front of Rose. "Is there anything else you'd particularly like?"

Before she could respond, a young man in a crisp ship's uniform stepped over. "Mrs. Devine," he said politely, "this came in to our communications office with explicit instructions that you sign and fax it back immediately."

Rose took the paper and held it up, but after only a moment, she sighed and set it down on the table. Raising her hands to her head, she rubbed her temples.

"Robert," she said gravely, "I need you to understand that I can only work with you if I'm one hundred per cent certain that you are always being straight with me. I will not waste one more second of my life wondering if what I'm getting from Danni's agent is *the truth, the whole truth and nothing but the truth.* Can you agree to this?"

This is it, dude, Sam thought, *this is your last chance with my mom.* Then, she caught Robert sneaking a quick peek in Abe's direction and Abe, in return, giving him back a quick, supportive nod. This completely blew Sam's mind: *Wowsa, Robert's looking to Grandpa Abe for support! That's so...human!*

Squaring his shoulders, Robert flashed his perfect smile. "Rose Devine, you have my word as a music agent and a gentleman that from this point forward, I shall only deal in absolute truths when taking care of you and yours."

Rose stood, shook his hand, picked up the fax, and shoved it into his chest. "Good. Tell me if I should sign this. I do *not* have the strength to deal with details this morning." She sat back down and sipped her coffee with an expression that seemed to Sam be one-part relief and two-parts pride in a situation well handled.

When Grandpa Abe finished eating, Olga and Sam escorted him back to the kennels. There they were greeted by a very happy Red. Sam sat on the ground and gave him lots of tickles. Olga checked out all the stuff that had been delivered to get Red primped and primed and prepared for his big public outing.

It took a long time for the girls to get the bath ready for Red; it took even longer to get him into it. Abe chuckled loudly as he watched the struggle.

Pushing from behind, Sam coaxed Red, "You want to make the best impression on everyone, don't you? There's going to be an *enormous* crowd up on deck and you'll be the only doggie, so everyone will be looking at you."

Abe's laughter vanished.

"How many persons are going to be on deck with us?" he asked. "I thought everyone would be getting off the ship and it would only be a handful of people left for the show. How big is this crowd we are going to be surrounded by?"

Sam shrugged. "Not sure. I heard Robert say something about six hundred seats with standing room for another two hundred." She craned her neck around. "Olga, did you hear how big they think the TV audience is going to be?"

"Somewhere between twelve and fourteen million," she answered.

"*People?* Twelve to fourteen million *people*," Abe echoed in disbelief.

Sam gave one huge push. Red went into the tub with an enormous splash. Sam and Olga grabbed him and scrubbed. After lathering, rinsing and repeating, the girls decided Red was clean enough. As tough as it had been getting the dog into the tub, getting him out was even harder. Finally, after twenty minutes of tugging and begging, Red hopped out and shook with all his might, sending water everywhere.

"Aw, Red," Sam whined. "Was that necessary?"

Red had so much hair that all the towels the girls had been given were completely soaked before the dog was even partially dry.

"I'll run to the laundry and get some more." Olga leaped up and left the room.

"Thanks!" Sam yelled out. She smacked her lips and realized she was getting hungry. "Hey, Grandpa Abe," she asked, while still focusing on Red, "want me to go grab snacks when Olga returns?"

There was no answer, so Sam twisted herself around

and was startled to see her grandfather staring sadly at the floor.

"Grandpa Abe?"

He lifted his hand to acknowledge he'd heard her, but didn't say a word.

Sam's worry level began to rise. "Are you all right?"

Without meeting her gaze, Abe answered, "I don't think we should take Red up to the show. It will be too hard on him. There will be too many people. He is an old dog. I will stay here with him."

"Aw, don't worry, Grandpa. It'll all be fine." Sam gave the dog a hug. "We'll all be there to watch out for him – me, Olga, Mom, even Robert."

Shaking his head, Abe's voice got more intense. "NO. You do not understand. It is *my* job to protect Red. I must take care of him and keep him safe. It is the least I can do."

"Why, Grandpa?" Sam asked. "Why? Why is it your job to protect Red? He's a dog. I thought it was the dog's job to protect his owner."

Abe's jaw tightened; his words came out slowly. "Samantha, you are still a young girl and still there are

some things that are too much for you. It is my job to protect my Red. That is that."

Her grandfather's harsh tone hurt Sam's feelings. Her first instinct was to bolt out of the kennel, but she paused to think. That thing Abe said about her being *still a girl* made her think that it wasn't anything bad about *her* directly: it was his own belief that she was only a little kid that was stopping him from opening up to her. The only way she'd ever get him to let down his guard and *really* talk to her about himself, his past, Golda, and the whole issue of Red's name, was to make him see her for the mature, almost-teenager that she knew she was inside.

Sam scooted over to her grandfather, flipped over a small bucket, plunked herself down on it, and sat up as tall as she could.

"Grandpa Abe," she said carefully, "it's true that I don't turn thirteen for two more weeks, but you have to know by now that I'm no baby. I understand a lot. I've read *The Diary of Anne Frank*. I know that not everything in life is fairy-tale perfect. I wish you'd have more faith in me. You're the closest thing I've ever had to speaking with my dad, and there's so much about you I still don't know and you won't tell me, and that is really hurting me. Please don't shut me out. I want to know more about you and your past, because then I'll know more about me and my past; then I can celebrate my own Day of the Dead and my own ancestors and where *my* smile comes from!" She paused to suck in a gulp of air. "Please talk to me!"

Grandpa Abe paused before slapping his hands down on his knees. "I did not recognize that I had caused such problems with my silence."

Sam tried to protest, but Abe hushed her.

"No, no, I do not mean that badly. I'm saying that it is I who have made a misstep by not sharing my stories. You and your mother and sister have been open with me; I want to return the trust of that openness."

Abe's eyes seemed to get fuzzy as he dug into his memory. He told his story unemotionally, as if he was remembering a movie he'd seen. He started at his beginning; he had been the only son in a small Polish family. When he was seven years old, the Nazi army had come in and taken control of Poland. The soldiers came to Abe's house; they said that since the Zabinskis were Jewish, they had to leave their house immediately

and move into an area of town called a ghetto. Abe's father didn't think it would be a safe place for his son, so he gave a man all his money to sneak little Abraham out of Poland and hide him somewhere safe.

Young Abe was frightened to go with the stranger, but he did exactly as his father instructed and went. The man took Abraham to a farm in Austria. There, he hid in the barn every day. Only at night could he step outside to stretch his legs and get the small portion of food the farmer's wife would leave out for him. Every now and then, she would also leave a book and little by little, Abe learned to read and speak German. Abe was always lonely. One night when he was sneaking out of the barn, he found himself in front of a dog, a mangey, skinny mutt. The dog snarled and blocked Abe's path to the farmhouse. It took all night, but eventually the dog allowed Abe to get round him. When he left to go back to the barn, Abe shared some of his meagre food with the creature. Eventually, the dirty, red dog came to trust Abe so much that he would snuggle and sleep with him all day and then walk beside him at night. Abe was grateful for the companionship and named him Mr. Red.

This was Abe's life for five whole years, until one night, when sneaking into the house, he heard on the radio that the Americans were near and the Nazi army was losing the war. It was then that his world changed again very suddenly.

One evening, while it was still light out, some Nazi soldiers came to the farm to take food from the farmer. Two soldiers entered the barn and were very close to finding Abe. He was so frightened he thought his heart would jump out of his chest. Just when the soldiers were about to see him, Red came running into the barn, barking as loud as he could. At first Abe thought that the dog was showing the soldiers exactly where he was hiding, but that wasn't the case at all. Red's barking kept the soldiers' attention on him at the front of the barn so Abe could sneak out the back! He managed to slip into the woods on the far side of the farm and planned to go back the next day to get Red. But an entire brigade of soldiers came to stay at the farm, so Abe couldn't get close enough to reach him! One day, the soldiers got bored and began firing their guns at the trees where Abe was hiding; it was then that Abe knew he had to leave for good.

It broke his heart to go without his beloved dog, but he had no choice.

After leaving the farm, Abe wandered and hid anywhere he could until he was discovered by a group of American soldiers. They took him to Germany to live in Föhrenwald, the displaced persons camp for Jewish orphans. At this point, Abe was almost thirteen years old, and since no family came to claim him, he ended up living in the camp for several years. It was there that he met and married Golda.

Gently, Abe looked into Sam's eyes. "Now you know the whole of it. This is why *I* must take care of Red; it is a life debt."

"But Grandpa Abe," Sam asked cautiously, "this isn't the same Red, right? Aside from the fact that *this* Red is *so not red*, he's not old. I mean, he's old, but he's not *that* old."

The familiar twinkle returned to Abe's eyes. "Ah, you mean he's not as *old* as your *ancient* grandpa here!" He laughed before continuing, "No, this is not the same Red, but I made a promise. Back when I could not get *the first* Mr. Red, I promised that for the rest of my life, I would always have a Red – a homeless dog

I would rescue and love and protect. This would forever be my way of thanking the original Mr. Red."

"I understand Grandpa, and I promise you that we will take super-special care of *this* Mr. Red. He will be totally protected and love being up on deck for Danni's show."

As Abe smiled, Olga walked back into the kennel with two hairdryers. "I thought it would be easier with these," she proudly proclaimed.

As the girls got to work getting Red dry and beautiful, Sam thought about her grandfather's story. She felt a stronger connection not only to Grandpa Abe, but also to her dad, her mom and Danni, now that she had a better understanding of how amazing it was that she had been able to bring her family together. Her thinking was interrupted by Robert's arrival.

"Hey. Hey!" He had to yell to be heard over the drone of the hairdryers. "Turn those off. I don't have time to shout at you today."

Sam rolled her eyes. *Nice to have the old Robert back,* she thought...*I guess.*

Robert waved his paper schedule in the air. "There has been a slight change of plan. Nothing we can't handle, but I'm going to need Abe sooner than planned." Softening his tone, Robert asked Abe, "If I helped you to your cabin now, could you be ready to join myself and Rose for a pre-concert interview? I know it's short notice, but we have a world-class reporter who wants to do a story on you. It would be excellent publicity for Danni and introduce her to a whole new audience. What do you think?"

Understanding exactly the worries that would be going through Abe's head, Sam looped her arm through her grandfather's. "We've got Red," she assured him. "Olga and I will take the very best care of him. We won't leave him alone for a minute. I promise you, Mr. Red will have an awesome afternoon. We'll meet you on deck for the concert. You can trust me, Grandpa."

Abe patted Sam on the head. "Yes, my dear," he said quietly, "I believe I can." He lifted his gaze to meet Robert's. "All right, Mr. Ruebens. I would be happy to join you for a chat with your reporter friend."

Robert held the kennel door open for Abe. Before leaving, the old man looked at his dog and softly said, "*Bądź grzeczny i nie proś Samanty o jedzenie.*"

"Grandpa," Sam called out, "what did you just say?"

Abe replied, "I tell him to be good and not to beg for treats."

Sam nodded; however, the minute Abe was out of sight, she pulled a small plastic bag out of her pocket. Crouching down next to the dog, she slyly fed him the three mushy sausages she'd snagged from the breakfast buffet.

"Here's the deal, my friend," she whispered into the dog's ear, "you keep taking care of my grandpa and I'll sneak you all the sausages you could ever dream of."

Red replied by giving Sam a wet, sloppy lick on the cheek.

"No matter what the rest of the world may think, at least you can feel confident that *somebody* loves you," Olga joked as she watched Sam wipe the slobber off her face.

Sam giggled, but then she thought of Danni and how tense she had been that morning. "Yup. I feel appreciated," she said. "Now let's hope my sister can say the same thing after tonight's big showdown!"

CHAPTER 20

Sam and Olga enjoyed their afternoon with Red.
They chilled, read magazines, and couldn't stop
complimenting each other on the amazing job they'd
done getting the old dog all clean and shiny. At 3.30,
the girls began trying to get Red buckled into his travel
harness for the concert, but getting him all strapped in
was pretty challenging.

Olga checked the time. "Sam, the officer will be
here in *thirty minutes* to take us to our seats."

Grunting in frustration, Sam nodded.

It took twenty more minutes, but both girls felt
victorious when they saw that they had succeeded and

all the straps were strapped and buckles buckled. Unfortunately, the second they high-fived each other, one of the buckles broke and popped off. Their smiles fell flat.

"Danni has a million shoes." Sam said as she leaped up. "One of them *has* to have a buckle!"

Olga grimaced. "Won't Danni be angry?"

"She'll never notice. Come on, we have to go *now*!"

When they reached their cabin, Olga stood outside with Red while Sam raced inside. She threw open the doors of Danni's closet and tore through a pile of footwear. It didn't take long before she found something that would work. She grabbed the shoe, ran back out to Olga, and held it up.

"What do you think?" she asked hopefully.

"I think it's fine," Olga answered. "But how are you going to attach it?"

Sam ran back inside. She returned with scissors and sticky tape. The business of cutting the buckle off Danni's shoe and securing it to Red's harness went pretty fast.

The buckle worked well enough, but it didn't look very good.

Sam groaned. "It's awful. Grandpa Abe is going to see that I broke Red's harness and think I'm a doofus."

"No," Olga said. "It's not *that* noticeable." She peeked at the clock in the cabin. "Yikes! The officer will be at the kennel for us in just a few minutes!"

Sam knew they couldn't be late, but the buckle looked awful. As she closed the cabin door, a red feathery scarf draped over a chair caught Sam's eye. She snagged it and ran to catch up with Olga and Red.

"This will work!" Sam shook the scarf. "It's the same colour as Red's harness!"

"Yeah," Olga agreed. "It's also the *same* as the goofy-looking boa that Inga was wearing back when you called her a giant red chicken."

Sam cracked up. "No wonder it seemed so familiar!"

Once they reached the kennels, Sam carefully wrapped the boa around Red's harness. It hid the taped-on buckle.

Sam scratched behind the dog's ears. "There we go! Now you're ready to party!"

The ship's officer arrived to take them up on deck.

"Stay close," he instructed as he placed plastic *VIP – All Access* passes around the necks of Sam, Olga and

Red. "I've never seen so many people on deck. It's pandemonium up there."

Walking up to the top deck was easy, but getting across it to the VIP section was total madness. As the officer slowly blazed a trail through the crowd, Sam held onto Red's harness so hard that she cut off the circulation in her hand. The horribly itchy pins-and-needles feeling that ensued hurt, but Sam was in charge of her grandfather's dog and she wasn't going to take *any* chances with him. For his part, Red didn't seem the least bit bothered by all the chaos.

After what seemed like an eternity of getting stepped on, smooshed and elbowed, they reached the VIP seating area. As the ship's officer held open the velvet rope for the girls and Red to pass through, Sam finally raised her head and saw the crazy scene unfolding all around her: helicopters buzzing around, television cameras moving into place, a girl on a megaphone shouting for everyone to take their seats – so much commotion that it made Sam feel dizzy. *It figures*, she thought. *Only when we're in the harbour do I get nauseated. With my luck, I'll end up barfing my guts out on live TV.*

"There!" Olga's voice snapped Sam back into the moment. "See your grandpa standing in the middle of the front row? Those must be our seats. Come on."

Sam followed Olga over to the centre of the front row where Robert was helping Abe get settled. Red barked and wagged his tail as he reached his beloved master. "Who is this handsome creature?" Abe asked. "What have you young ladies done with my messy dog?"

Both girls beamed with pride.

Robert glanced down at his watch. "Abe, I need to be backstage. Can I order you anything before I leave – a bottle of water, a can of soda?"

"No, thank you," he replied. "You have done more than enough al—"

Grandpa Abe was interrupted by the sudden noisy appearance of Jean and Jehan. The twins were squabbling and drawing quite a bit of attention to themselves.

"Robert!" The brother dressed in black threw his hands in the air. "Would you please explain to my foolish twin 'ere zat against ze evening sky, Danni must only be in shades of aqua, not teal as he wrongly insists?"

The other brother, the one in brown, wagged his

finger in the air. "No! Robert, explain to my idiotic twin zat ze placement of ze stage lights 'ere demands only teals on Danni; no aquas, no!"

"Jehan! Jean! *Gentlemen!*" Robert raised his voice to get control.

The bickering brothers hushed up by covering their mouths with their hands.

"Good," Robert continued. "Let's discuss this *backstage*, please."

Nodding in unison, the brothers began to float away, but the one dressed in black suddenly stopped. He stared at Red.

"Sam?" He kept his gaze fixed on the dog. "What eez zat doggie wearing around iz neck?"

"That red thing?" She pointed. "That's his travel harness."

The twin crossed his arms in front of his body. "No, not zat. I'm asking about ze feathers around iz neck."

Sam replied, "*Oh.* It's some old scarf I snagged from Danni's room."

"Zat is not *some old scarf*!" The brother's face turned scarlet. "Zat eez ze boa *I* gave Danni early zis morning as a break-a-leg gift for ze concert tonight!"

He angrily unwrapped it from the harness, threw it around his own neck, and stormed off, leaving a trail of red feathers behind him.

Sam wanted to chase after him and apologize, but before she could, the lights surrounding the stage flipped on and the crowd roared with excitement. The whole ship seemed to shake with energy. The announcer's voice boomed out from the enormous speakers. He pumped up the crowd by getting the rival fan clubs to try to out-cheer each other. While this went on, Sam wondered if she should say something to Grandpa Abe about his big surprise song coming at the end of the show. She didn't want to ruin it by telling Abe exactly which song Danni would be singing in his honour, but she was tempted to let him know that something amazing was waiting for him. As she struggled with this, the announcer introduced Danni and Harley. The two pop rivals walked out from opposite sides of the stage and met in the centre. A dancer wearing a referee costume joined them and flipped a coin. Danni called *heads*; when the coin landed heads up, she elected to have Harley go first.

Over the next ninety minutes, each singer

performed three songs in a row before turning the stage over to the other girl. Even though their styles were completely different, both Harley and Danni were mind-blowingly amazing. They sang and danced at the top of their abilities, knocking the socks off everybody in the audience. By the intermission, even the most die-hard fans had to admit that *both* entertainers were putting on one of the most amazing concerts anyone had ever witnessed.

Sam glanced over at Grandpa Abe to see what he thought of the concert. The smile on his face made it clear that he was enjoying himself.

"Now I understand why your sister is famous. If I could sing and dance like that, I would be on the television too." He chuckled at the thought. "Not that I could imagine anyone paying money to see these old legs doing any fancy moves."

Even though she teehee-d along with Grandpa's joke, Sam's mind was now completely focused on Danni singing "Pennies From Heaven". She *so badly* wanted to say something, because she couldn't wait to see the smile on Grandpa Abe's face when he heard the music. But what if hearing the song made him all *sad*?

Oh man! What if her great surprise turned out to be a massive dud and she made her grandfather cry? Sam began to pull on her hair as she struggled with her fears of impending doom.

"You okay?" Olga asked quietly.

Sam nodded, but her stomach was spinning hard core. *I blew it*, she thought. *I should have asked if he would have liked to hear Golda's song. If this surprise is too much for him and he ends up all bummed out because I sprang it on him, I'll never forgive myself.*

Even though she tried to enjoy the rest of the concert, Sam couldn't completely get those panicky feelings out of her head. She didn't even bother watching Harley as she performed her last set of songs and barely looked up at Danni during her last three numbers. Instead, she kept glancing at Grandpa Abe out of the corner of her eye.

Harley's big finale was pretty darned spectacular. She had wicked fireworks shooting off around her as she wildly ripped on her guitar. Even Sam had to admit that Harley had proved she was a talented musician.

As Harley was taking her final bows, Sam caught a glimpse of her sister, waiting just offstage. The twins were with her. The brother in brown brushed powder on Danni's nose, while the brother in black fussed with the back of her miniskirt. *This is it, Danni,* Sam thought, *this is your ultimate opportunity to prove to all those people who've been bad-mouthing you the last few months that you really and truly are the Number One Pop Superstar on Planet Earth!*

Danni took one last sip of water and prepared to step out onto the stage for her big finale, but in that very last second, as she took in a deep breath and straightened herself to stand as tall as she possibly could, something caught her eye and caused her to turn her head. She reached out and grabbed something. Sam gasped when she realized what she was witnessing; Danni had grabbed the red boa from the shoulders of Jean – or Jehan – from *one* of the twins, and wrapped it around her neck as she strode confidently out to the pink spotlight where a stool and an old-fashioned microphone were waiting for her in the centre of the stage.

No, Sam screamed inside, *NO!* She tried to scream out loud, but panic gripped her so hard that no sound could escape her throat. She jumped out of her seat and waved her arms in the hope of warning her sister about the boa having been around Red. Unfortunately, Sam's gyrations were useless because by the time Danni reached the spotlight and could see the audience, *everyone* was on their feet cheering for her.

In that pink spotlight, Danni appeared to be the picture-perfect definition of a pop superstar. Her sparkly outfit shimmered, her glossy hair shone, but all Sam could concentrate on was the horrible red boa. To the rest of the audience, it may have appeared to be a funky accessory; to Sam, it was a ticking time bomb.

"I dedicate my last number tonight," Danni's lovely voice rang out, "to a very special person. A man I haven't known for a long time, but someone without whom I wouldn't be here tonight." She giggled. "And I really do mean that, because I'm talking about my grandfather, Grandpa Abe! This song was my grandmother's favourite, and I hope you'll find it as special as I do: 'Pennies From Heaven'!"

The band began to play the beautiful, haunting melody. Danni swayed, waiting for her cue. *It'll be okay*, Sam thought, *she's had the boa around her neck for a couple of minutes, and so far, so good. Maybe her*

allergies aren't that bad. Maybe she isn't really all that allergic to dogs.

Uh-oh.

Sam watched in horror as Danni's face began to turn blotchy and she reached up to rub her neck; it was exactly what had happened at Grandpa Abe's just before she launched into a full-scale, throat-closing allergy attack. Danni shook her head and tried to swallow, but it was becoming apparent that something was wrong. A couple of little coughs gave way to several desperate gasps for breath. By this point, the band had stopped playing, restarted the song, and then stopped again. The entire ship was stone-cold silent. All eyes were on Danni, except Sam's; as soon as she saw her sister struggle to get air into her lungs, she ran over to the steps on the side of the stage. Bounding onto the huge platform, Sam grabbed the boa, yanked it off her sister, and threw it to the floor.

"Mom!" Sam cried out to Rose, who was frozen with confusion in the wings. "Mom! It's an allergy attack. Danni needs her medicine and some water."

Rose and Robert quickly scooted over. They half-walked, half-carried Danni offstage. Sam bit her

bottom lip as she watched them exit stage left. Trying not to cry, she closed her eyes and let her head fall forward, her chin resting on her chest. She hoped desperately that her sister would soon be back to normal and that nobody in the family would blame her for the horrible mess, but she would understand if they did. After all, it was pretty embarrassing for Danni to have such a terrible allergy attack in front of the crowd on the ship and millions of people watching on live television as she launched into her big, final, super-special song.

The concert? THE CONCERT! Sam's eyes flew open; her head snapped up as she realized that all those people who had been staring at her sister were now staring at *her*! There she was, alone, in the centre of the stage, with something like a zillion people watching her, and she was clueless. She sighed loudly, but jumped back half a second later when the sound of it was picked up by the microphone in front of her.

She looked to her right and saw Rose and Robert caring for Danni. *Okay*, she thought, *that's good.* But her relief popped like a balloon when she glanced over to her left and saw Harley and her manager standing,

 301

watching, waiting. Furiously, Sam reached out and grabbed the microphone thinking, *I'll show them!*

Sam's moment of confidence flew out of the window as soon as she looked out at the live audience. With the spotlight in her eyes, she couldn't see the crowd's individual faces, but she sure could see the outlines of all those hundreds of heads looking her way, waiting for her to say something.

"Hi."

The word echoed several times, each one sounding lamer than the previous.

"I...I'm Sam, Danni's sister, and...she's going to be fine. She's having a bad allergy attack. It's kind of my... it *is* my fault, and I'm really sorry. I convinced Danni to do something really special for our grandpa and..." Sam's voice trailed off as she heard it bounce around the deck. *I sound like a loser*, she thought.

The crowd grew restless. Sam heard grumbling and rumbling. She gritted her teeth. *Pull it together, girl! You have to save this for Danni and Grandpa Abe!*

"See..." Sam threw her hands out in front of her. "I'm *so* not a pop star! *Danni* is the singer in the family.

This big surprise for our grandpa…I can't do it. If you just wait a couple of minutes, I'm sure…"

Sam stopped speaking when she heard boos and whistles from the audience. It was just a few people at first, but it wasn't long before more joined in.

"Please," Sam pleaded, "please hang on. If you could be patient and give Danni a couple more minutes to get through this allergy thing, I promise it'll be worth it!"

The negative reactions from the crowd grew even louder. Desperate to figure out a way to buy her sister enough time to return triumphantly to the stage, Sam rubbed her nose, and thought so hard she felt her skull would explode.

Decide what kind of person you want to be, and make decisions to act that way. Grandpa Abe's words buzzed around her brain. *Okay, I can do this.*

With her eyes tightly closed, Sam reached forward, pulled the microphone close to her mouth, and began to sing "Pennies From Heaven". It took the audience a couple of seconds to pipe down and listen, and only a couple more seconds to recognize that Sam had been telling the truth – she was *seriously* not a pop star. Her

warbling was awful. There was some giggling and a few snarky comments, but generally, the audience was stunned silent.

Sam had to focus with all her might to remember the words. She knew she wasn't sounding very good, but kept going because she wasn't singing for herself, she was singing for her grandpa, her sister, and all those fans who'd stood by Danni when Harley and her groupies called Danni a second-rater. Sam's attention was so directed on getting through the song that she didn't feel the hand tapping on her shoulder.

After several gentle taps, the hand poked Sam's arm, but even that didn't wake Sam out of her steadfastness. Finally, the hand whacked Sam on the side of her head. *That* got her attention.

"*Hey*," Sam whined as she rubbed the sore spot. "What's the—"

Seeing Harley standing next to her was honestly the last thing Sam ever expected, but there she was.

"You got guts, kid." Harley leaned close to Sam. "*No* musical ability whatsoever, but major league guts."

* * *

Click click click, clack clack click.

OMG!

Danni's finale *totally delivered* on *the* surprise of the evening, but it wasn't the one we'd planned.

I was the one in the spotlight trying to sing the song for Grandpa Abe (don't ask — the details are too painful) when suddenly Harley — yes, HARLEY — came to my rescue!

She shouted for everyone to "zip it"! It worked; the entire ship went silent. Then she told the audience that the whole *battleship* theme of the concert was "stupid" and that SHE was a huge Danni Devine fan herself. Harley said how sorry she was for all the rotten things she'd said about Danni and me. And as if that wasn't brain-bending enough, she asked me if she could HELP with the special surprise for Grandpa Abe. I was totally tongue-tied so I nodded and backed out of her way.

Harley struck a chord on her electric guitar before saying, "Grandpa Abe, dude, you are a real gentleman, and this here classy song is for you."

And then she launched into this mind-blowing version of "Pennies From Heaven"! The audience went insane! As Harley rocked out, Danni recovered from her allergy attack. She watched the performance from the side of the stage. Harley saw her and motioned for her to come out. Danni waved her off, but Harley insisted, so Danni did and they finished the song TOGETHER (which worked out *super* well because I don't think Harley knew all the words to the song)! It was the most off-the-charts finale EVER! The crowd roared so loud that I'm sure they heard it back in England.

As Harley and Danni took their bows, I looked around; Mom was beaming with pride, and on Grandpa Abe's face was the most beautiful smile I'd ever seen. My throat got all scratchy with

emotion; when I reached up to rub it, I felt the chain around my neck, the one with my grandma's wedding ring on it. I know this sounds corny...but for one *perfect moment*, I felt like I had my whole family around me, and that felt even better than being out in a field, at sunset, eating a waffle cone filled with chocolate-chip-cookie-dough ice cream, while riding my very own horse and having Olga riding her horse right next to me!

More soon (but seriously – how can I ever write anything that'll top this???)

CHAPTER 21

Sam's thirteenth birthday *couldn't* have started out any better. Danni and Rose woke her by bursting into her room and singing "Happy Birthday" at the tops of their voices. After a perfect breakfast of chocolate-chip pancakes with peanut butter and maple syrup, she grabbed her bike and headed out for the stables. Her entire day was spent with Olga, riding their favourite horses around the hills and valleys of the SuAn Stables.

As the sun set, the girls rode back to the barn. After feeding and brushing down their horses, Olga suggested they stop for a soda at the stables' outdoor picnic area before going home.

Sam followed her friend. She wasn't really paying attention; her brain was busy blissfully musing over how much fun she'd had riding all day. When she stepped into the picnic area, a loud noise startled her. It took a second for her to recognize she'd just heard her family yelling, "Surprise!"

Sam joyfully noticed that the entire picnic area had been decorated for her. There were strings of coloured lights, a real country-and-western fiddle player, and a roaring campfire.

Rose, wearing the pinkest cowgirl outfit and the highest-heeled boots Sam had ever seen, threw open her arms. "Come on in, pardners," she crowed, "I think ya'll will be liking the vittles we've cooked up special for ya."

Glancing around, Sam couldn't contain her glee and giggled at the sight of her mom, sister, grandpa, Red and even Robert sitting around the campfire in their cowboy hats. "Mom, this is too cool! I had *no* clue. You really got me!"

With an exaggerated tip of her hat, Rose replied, "Why, thank ya, little lady."

* * *

Click click click, clack clack click.

My thirteenth birthday was a hoot and a half! I got to do all my favourite things: ride horses, hang with my best friend and family, and eat like there was no tomorrow!

At my AWESOME surprise party, Mom sat next to me on a bale of hay and handed me a letter. As I read it, I thought it was one of those totally emotional letters designed to make the reader bawl out loud. I was half right. The first part of the letter did get me all misty; it mentioned how proud Mom is of the young lady I've become and all that kind of stuff. However, instead of staying all mushy, the letter announced how Mom had booked a whole week at a ranch in Montana! A WHOLE WEEK OF RIDING HORSES AND CAMPING OUT UNDER THE STARS! I can't wait! Olga (who is *so* invited!) is as excited as me.

Then Grandpa Abe handed me a box and said it was a gift from both him and Red. A robot dog!

A totally awesome RED robot dog! I can't tell you how much I love it! It barks and learns commands and follows the sound of my voice! Grandpa Abe explained how he and Red wanted me to know that even though we live far apart, we would never again be truly separated since we now had a solid family bond, and my little robot doggie was a way to always remember that…*without* making Danni ill.

After my party, it was time to say goodbye to Grandpa Abe and Red. I had to fight with myself not to bawl my eyes out. Really and truly. I'd have given anything for them to stay; but I understood. Grandpa has his own home and his own life back in England. Plus, this way, I have the best excuse EVER for going back to London every summer!

Oh! I never told you how the whole Danni versus Harley thing worked out. It's totally amazing — after the big finale on the ship, where Harley and Danni sang "Pennies From Heaven" together, Harley hung out with our family backstage. She

apologized for all the horrible things she'd said and explained that she'd only done that because her manager had told her it would be good for her career! He said that Danni would know it was just a publicity stunt, so she wouldn't take any of the nastiness seriously. When Danni told her how much pain the barbs had caused her, Harley got angry. REALLY angry! She fired her manager on the spot and hired Robert! She and Danni talk on the phone all the time now. It sounds like they're trying to arrange a tour together next summer. That would be too cool — I could spend part of next summer in England with Grandpa Abe and Red, and the rest on tour with Danni and Harley. Would that not be the greatest summer EVER?!?!

It's beyond-words-wonderful having my happy sister back again. See, a happy *Danni* makes for a happy *Mom* and a happy *Mom* lets *me* be a very happy Sam!

Hmm…speaking of happy Sam…I was very happy tonight pigging out on birthday cake. Time

to end this blog and sneak downstairs for a little more (hopefully, a corner piece with a ton of icing).

Ciao for now!

Sam hit "post", rose from her chair, and headed towards the door.

"Not so fast there, Miss Thing." Blu's voice echoed through her bedroom.

As the bedroom wall mirror slowly slid up, it revealed first the feet, then the legs, next the arms, and then the goofy grin of her favourite, dreadlocked, reality TV director.

"Where do you think you're going?" he asked.

"To the kitchen to sneak a little more birthday cake. You want some?"

Blu cackled. "Boring old birthday cake! I think not!" He stepped aside and threw his arms out to reveal a giant cupcake, complete with birthday candle. "Ta-dah!"

Sam snorted. "I've never seen anybody get so excited over a cupcake before."

"Well, excuse me, *Jamie Oliver*, but this is not just *any* cupcake. This is *my* world-famous chocolate-cream-cheese cupcake. And, as amazing as it is, it'll taste even better when you learn that once you finish it, you get your birthday present!" Blu sat down in his chair. "Of course, if you aren't interested, I'll eat it myself and shelve the present."

"No! *No!*" Sam sprang forward. "I love cupcakes! I love presents!"

Blu laughed. "Oh, all right." He slapped the stool next to him. "Come on in!"

Stepping into the control room, Sam waited for her eyes to adjust to the glare from all the monitors. She made her way over to the stool next to Blu.

"Phew," she said with relief, "I actually made it without tripping over any cables."

"This really *is* a special day!" Blu kidded her.

Sam slugged him on the arm. After she made a wish and blew out the candle, the two joked and laughed as she scoffed the wickedly tasty cupcake.

Once every last crumb was gone, Blu spun around in his chair and began fiddling with the buttons and levers on the huge machine in front of him.

Sam, waiting for her birthday present, watched him for a bit before asking, "What are you doing?"

Blu didn't answer. He kept his focus on manipulating the giant machine. Sam pestered him again.

"Blu? Hello? What are you doing?"

"Hang on!" Blu shouted. "I'm almost ready with your rockin' hot birthday gift." He hit a large green button in the middle of the main panel and then spun his chair to face her. "Here we go! In honour of this momentous occasion – it's not every day you officially become a teenager, you know – I'm giving you the once-in-a-lifetime opportunity to be the *director* for our special hour-long episode of *The Devine Life* – the one that covers your trip to London and the concert with Harley."

Sam's jaw dropped. "No!" she exclaimed. "*Me?* You're going to let *me* make the TV show the way *I* want it? You'd give me the opportunity to finally get to show my family to the world the way *I* see them? Really-truly?"

"Really-truly!" Spreading his arms out wide, Blu announced, "Madame Director, you are in charge; I am at your command."

 315

And the two friends worked until the wee hours of the morning, laughing, drinking orange cream soda, burping, and putting together the absolute best episode of *The Devine Life* – EVER.

A few things you didn't know about KIMBERLY GREENE

Which five words would you use to describe yourself?

☆ Loyal

☆ Goofy

☆ Happy

☆ Creative

☆ ~~Short~~ Petite!

How do you spend a typical day?

Since becoming a mommy, I don't really have typical days any more. However, I still do walk the dogs (and the baby) over to the Coffee Bean every morning so I can get my Blueberry-Pomegranate Tea Latte (oh-so-good!). After that, every day is a race to get work done (writing, teaching, helping students) while still taking care of my little boy (changing diapers, playing games, singing songs, avoiding the flying food). The days go by so fast that before I get a chance to think about it, it's night and I'm getting the baby ready for bed. Now that I'm looking at this, I'm thinking – hey, I need a vacation!

☆ How do you write?

More than ever, writing is pure joy for me because it's about the only real "me time" I get. It has to be only in spits 'n' spurts because the baby only naps for so long – but that's okay.

☆ What is your ideal way to spend a day off?

There are no days off for a new mom. :-) But if I did manage one, I'd want to go skiing. I miss it mucho, mucho, mucho!

☆ What would you be if you weren't a writer?

I'd be less exhausted because I'd get a lot more sleep (LOL).

☆ What's on your iPod?

Where to begin??? How's this for a hint of what a musical nutbar I am...

- ☆ Crib Disco – disco music redone with soft tones for the baby (totally hilarious)
- ☆ Podcasts of *Sesame Street*
- ☆ Hollaback Girl (dance mix) – Gwen Stefani
- ☆ Abba! Even when I'm super-exhausted, these songs get me up and out the door (great for when I'm running)

Check out
WWW.FICTION.USBORNE.COM
for more STAR-STUDDED reads!